"What's wrong?"

Halle shrugged. "You know when it feels like someone is watching you? Maybe it was my imagination."

Liam opened her door for her. She stared at him a moment, then said, "Thanks."

He climbed in and fastened his seat belt. There was another question burning in his brain. "Were you considering writing a book about Andy's disappearance?"

"I'd thought about it, but the time never seemed right. Some part of me thought maybe if I put all my thoughts and memories into a book, maybe if he was out there somewhere he would read it and remember. He would know we hadn't forgotten him and that we still love him."

He stared at her profile as she moved her foot from the brake to the accelerator and the car rolled forward. The line of her jaw, the rise of her cheekbones, her lips, her nose—all of it filled him with a sudden sense of longing. How would it feel to have someone love you that much? His heart started pounding.

He understood how it would feel. It would feel exactly like this.

BEFORE HE VANISHED

USA TODAY Bestselling Author
DEBRA WEBB

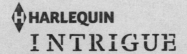

This book is dedicated to the many, many children who go missing every day and the determined folks who work so hard to find them.

ISBN-13: 978-1-335-13633-6

Before He Vanished

Copyright © 2020 by Debra Webb

Recycling programs for this product may not exist in your area.

This edition published by arrangement with Harlequin Books S.A.

For questions and comments about the quality of this book, please contact us at CustomerService@Harlequin.com.

Harlequin Enterprises ULC
22 Adelaide St. West, 40th Floor
Toronto, Ontario M5H 4E3, Canada
www.Harlequin.com

Printed in U.S.A.

Debra Webb is the award-winning *USA TODAY* bestselling author of more than one hundred novels, including those in reader-favorite series Faces of Evil, the Colby Agency and Shades of Death. With more than four million books sold in numerous languages and countries, Debra has a love of storytelling that goes back to her childhood on a farm in Alabama. Visit Debra at www.debrawebb.com.

Books by Debra Webb

Harlequin Intrigue

A Winchester, Tennessee Thriller

In Self Defense
The Dark Woods
The Stranger Next Door
The Safest Lies
Witness Protection Widow
Before He Vanished

Colby Agency: Sexi-ER

Finding the Edge
Sin and Bone
Body of Evidence

Faces of Evil

Dark Whispers
Still Waters

Colby Agency: The Specialists

Bridal Armor
Ready, Aim...I Do!

Colby, TX

Colby Law
High Noon
Colby Roundup

Debra Webb writing with Regan Black

Harlequin Intrigue

Colby Agency: Family Secrets

Gunning for the Groom

The Specialists: Heroes Next Door

The Hunk Next Door
Heart of a Hero
To Honor and To Protect
Her Undercover Defender

Visit the Author Profile page at Harlequin.com.

CAST OF CHARACTERS

Halle Lane—Her career in Nashville took a dive; now she's Winchester's hotshot new investigative reporter. But can she find the truth about her neighbor and best friend who disappeared twenty-five years ago?

Liam Hart—His life is as close to perfect as can be. He owns a beautiful vineyard that his father started before he was born. When a newspaper article questions all that he believes to be true, he has no choice but to find a way to dispel the lies...or find the truth.

Nancy Clark—Her son, Andy, Halle's best friend, went missing when he was seven. With the news of her cancer, Nancy believes it's time everyone knew the truth.

Penelope Hart—Since Liam's father passed away, his stepmother hasn't been around much. What is she avoiding or hiding from?

Claire Hart—Claire adores her older brother. She is determined to help him solve this mystery.

Chief of Police William Brannigan—The top cop in Winchester; he will not stop until he solves the newest crime in his town.

Chapter One

NOW

Friday, March 6
Winchester, Tennessee

Halle Lane listened as her fellow newspaper reporter droned on and on about the upcoming community events in Winchester that he planned to cover, which was basically everything on the calendar for the next month.

She couldn't really complain. Halle was new. Hardly ninety days on the job, but she knew Winchester every bit as well as Mr. Roger Hawkins. She couldn't bring herself to call him Rog. The man was seventy if he was a day and he'd covered the social events of Winchester for about fifty of those years.

How could she—a fading-star investigative journalist from Nashville—expect to get first dibs on anything in Winchester? Hawkins had the social events, including obituaries. Her boss and the owner of the newspaper, Audrey Anderson-Tanner, generally took care of the big stories. The only potential for a break in the monotony of covering barroom brawls and petty break-ins was the fact that Audrey was pregnant. At nearly thirty-eight, she was expecting her first child.

Halle had wanted to jump for joy when she heard the news last month. She was, of course, very happy for Audrey and her husband, Sheriff Colt Tanner, but mostly she was thrilled at the idea that she might actually get her hands on a real story sometime this decade.

So far that had not happened. Audrey had covered the big federal trial of Harrison Armone last month. His son's widow, the sole witness against him, had been hiding out in Winchester for months. Surprisingly for such a small town, Winchester had more than its share of big news happenings. This time last year a body had been discovered in the basement of this very newspaper building. Halle's gaze shifted to the head of the conference table, where her boss listened with seemingly rapt interest as Hawkins went on and on.

It seemed Winchester also had more than its share of family secrets, as well. A man posing as a Mennonite had turned out to be a former member of a Chicago mob. Not a month later, Sasha Lenoir-Holloway had uncovered the truth about the deaths of her parents. Cece Winters had come home from prison a few months back and blown open the truth about her family and the cult-like extremists living in a remote area of Franklin County.

Nashville had nothing on Winchester, it seemed.

"This all sounds good, Rog," Audrey said, her voice pulling Halle back to the here and now.

The boss's gaze shifted to her and Halle realized her mistake. She had been silently bemoaning all the stories she'd missed and now it was her turn to share with those gathered what she was working on for this week's Sunday edition.

"Halle, what do you have planned?" Audrey asked.

For five endless seconds she racked her brain for something, anything to say.

Then her gaze landed on the date written in black across the white board.

March 6.

Memories whispered through her mind. Voices and images from her childhood flooded her senses. Blond hair, blue eyes…

"The lost boy," Halle said in a rush. The words had her heart pounding.

Of course. Why hadn't she thought of that last month or the month before?

Audrey frowned for a moment, then made an "aha" face. "Excellent idea. We've just passed what? Twenty-four years?"

"Twenty-five," Halle confirmed. "Andy Clark

was my neighbor. We played together all the time as kids."

Brian Peterson, the editor of the *Winchester Gazette*, chimed in next. "What makes you think Nancy Clark will allow an interview? She hasn't in all these years."

Audrey made a frustrated face. "That is true. You tried to interview her for both the ten-year and the twenty-year anniversaries, didn't you?"

Brian nodded. "I did. She refused to talk about it. Since her husband passed away year before last, she's practically a shut-in. She stopped attending church. Has whatever she needs delivered." He shrugged, shifted his attention to Halle. "Good luck with that one."

Halle's anticipation deflated. Hawkins looked at her as if she were something to be pitied.

"Still," Audrey said, "if you could get the story, it would be huge. Maybe since you and the boy, Andy, played together as children before he vanished, she might just talk to you."

Halle's hopes lifted once more. "I'm certain she will."

The conference room started to buzz with excitement. Titles were tossed about. Potential placement on the front page above the fold.

All Halle had to do was make it happen.

HALLE CRUISED ALONG the street on the east side of the courthouse, braking at a crosswalk for a mother pushing a stroller. That little ache that pricked each time she saw a baby did so now. Passing thirty had flipped some switch that had her yearning for a child of her own.

Now that she was back home, her chances of finding a partner, much less having a child, had dropped to something less than zero.

Winchester was a very small town compared to Nashville. With a population of around ten thousand, if you counted Decherd in the mix, it truly was the sort of place where everyone knew everyone else.

There were times when this could be a very good thing. Like when Andy Clark went missing twenty-five years ago. Halle had been just a little kid, but she remembered well how citizens from all over this county as well as those surrounding it had rushed to help look for Andy. Headlines about "the lost boy" scrolled across every newspaper in the state. His face was all over the news. Detectives and FBI agents were in and out of the Clark home for months.

But Andy had vanished without a trace.

Halle turned onto South High Street. The Clark home was on the corner of South High and Sixth Avenue. The historic Victorian was among the town's oldest homes. A meticulously manicured lawn and sprawling front porch greeted visitors. She pulled to the curb in front of the house and shut off the engine. The ancient maple on the Sixth Avenue side of the lawn had been Andy's and her favorite climbing tree.

Next door was Halle's childhood home. Her parents, Judith and Howard, had been thrilled when she'd announced last Christmas that she would be moving back to Winchester. They had, of course, insisted that she move back into her old room. As much as she appreciated the offer and adored her parents, that was not happening. Eventually the two had talked her into taking the apartment over the detached garage where her Aunt Daisy, the old maid everyone always whispered about, had once lived, God rest her soul.

Considering she would have her own parking spot and a separate entrance, Halle decided it wasn't such a bad idea. She would have her privacy and her parents would have their only daughter—only child, actually—living at home again.

A win-win for all involved. As long as she didn't dwell on the fact that she had turned thirty-two at the end of last month and that her one and only marriage had ended in divorce two years ago or that her ex-husband had since remarried and had a child—no matter that he had said they were too young for children when she had wanted one.

Not.

Maybe the garage apartment was fitting considering her mother's peers all now whispered about her unmarried status. *Bless her heart, she's like poor Daisy.*

Halle heaved a weary sigh.

The divorce had turned her world upside down, shaken her as nothing ever had. She'd lost her footing, and the upheaval had shown in her work. Just as she'd begun to pull her professional self together again, she'd been let go. Cutbacks, they had said. But she'd known the truth. Her work had sucked for two years.

It was a flat-out miracle they had allowed her to keep working as long as they had.

Luckily for Halle, Audrey was open to second chances. She had understood how one's life could go completely awry. Though the *Winchester Gazette* was only a small biweekly newspaper, it was a reasonable starting place to rebuild Halle's career.

She climbed out of the car, draped her leather bag over her shoulder and closed the door. The midmorning air was crisp but Halle much preferred it to what would come between June and September. The melting heat and suffocating humidity. The not-so-pleasant part of Southern living.

Stepping up onto the porch, she heard the swing chains squeak as the breeze nudged this wooden mainstay of every Southern porch gently back and forth. On the other end of the sprawling outdoor space stood a metal glider, still sporting its original green paint, offering a restful place to sit and watch the street. But Mrs. Clark never sat on her porch anymore. Halle's mother had said the lady rarely stepped out the door, just as Brian had also mentioned. But Mrs. Clark did come to the door as long as she could identify the person knocking or ringing her bell. Whether she opened the door was another story.

Halle hadn't attempted to visit her in years. She was relatively certain she hadn't seen the woman since her husband's funeral two years ago. The one thing Halle never had to worry about was being recognized. With her fiery mass of unruly red curls, the impossible-to-camouflage freckles and the mossy green eyes, folks rarely forgot her face. The other kids in school had been ruthless with the ginger-and-carrottop jokes but Andy had always defended her…at least until he was gone.

God, she had missed her best friend. Even at seven, losing your best friend was incredibly traumatic.

Halle stepped to the door and lifted her fist and knocked.

"What do you want?"

The voice behind the closed door was a little rusty, as if it wasn't used often, but it was reasonably strong.

"Mrs. Clark, you might not remember me—"

"Of course I remember you. What do you want?"

It was a starting place.

"Ma'am, may I come inside and speak with you?" She bit her bottom lip and searched for a good reason. "It's a little chilly here on the porch." Not exactly true, but not entirely a lie.

A latch clicked. Anticipation caught her breath. Another click and the knob turned. The door drew inward a couple of feet. Nancy Clark stood in the shadows beyond the reach of daylight. Her hair looked as unruly as Halle's and it was as white as cotton. She was shorter than Halle remembered.

"Come in."

The door drew inward a little more and Halle crossed the threshold. Her heart was really pumping now. She reminded herself that just because she was inside didn't mean she would manage an interview.

One step at a time, Hal.

The elderly lady closed the door and locked it. So maybe she anticipated Halle staying awhile. Another good sign.

"I was having tea in the kitchen," that rusty voice said.

When she turned and headed deeper into the gloom of the house, Halle followed. She knew this house as well as she knew her own. Until she was seven years old it had been her second home. More of those childhood memories whispered through her, even ones her mother had told her about before Halle was old enough to retain the images herself.

Her mother had laughed and recounted to her the many times she'd had tea with Nancy while the babies toddled around the kitchen floor. The Clarks had not always lived in Winchester, Halle's mother had told her. They had bought the house when their little boy was two years old, just before Easter. Judith Lane had been thrilled to have a neighbor with a child around the same age as her own. Halle had been twenty months old. Even the fathers, Howard and Andrew, had become fast friends.

It was perfect for five years.

Then Andy disappeared.

The shriek of the kettle yanked Halle's attention back to the present.

"You want cream?"

"That would be nice." She forced a smile into place as she stood in the kitchen watching Mrs. Clark fix the tea.

Nancy prepared their tea in classic bone china patterned with clusters of pink flowers ringing the cups. She placed the cups in their saucers and then onto a tray. She added the matching cream pitcher and sugar bowl.

Halle held her breath as the elderly woman with her tiny birdlike arms carried the tray to the dining table. To be back in this home, after so many years, to be talking with this woman who'd occupied a special place in her heart because of her relationship to Andy was enough to make Halle feel lightheaded.

"Get the cookies," Nancy called over her shoulder.

Halle turned back to the counter and picked up the small plate, then followed the same path the lady had taken. They sat, added sugar to their tea and then tested the taste and heat level. Mrs. Clark offered the plate of cookies and Halle took a small one and nibbled.

Rather than rush the conversation, she reacquainted herself with the paintings and photographs on the wall. Beyond the wide doorway, she could see the stunning painting over the fireplace in the main parlor. Andy had been five at the time. His hair had been so blond, his eyes so blue. Such a sweet and handsome boy. She hadn't a clue about what handsome even was or any of that stuff back then; she had only known that she loved him like another part of her family…of herself. They had been inseparable.

"Twenty-five years."

Halle's attention swung to the woman who sat at the other end of the table. She looked so frail, so small. The many wrinkles on her face spoke of more than age. They spoke of immense pain, harrowing devastation. Worrying for twenty-five long years if her child was alive. If he had been tortured and murdered.

If she would ever see him again.

"Yes, ma'am," Halle agreed.

Nancy Clark set her tea cup down and placed her palms flat on the table. "You want to write an article about him, don't you?"

Halle dared to nod, her heart pounding. This was the moment of truth. Would she be able to persuade Mrs. Clark to open up to her, to give her the answers she needed as much for the story as for her own peace of mind? "It would mean a great deal to me."

"If you've done your homework, you're aware I've never given an interview. Nor did my Andrew."

"I am and I understand why."

Her head angled ever so slightly as she stared down the table at Halle. "Really? What is it you think you understand?"

Halle nodded. "How can you adequately articulate that kind of loss? That sort of pain? You loved him more than anything in this world and someone took him from you. How could you possibly find the right words?"

Mrs. Clark's gaze fell first, then her head bowed.

Halle held her breath. Whether the lady believed her or agreed with her, Halle did understand. She had loved Andy, too, and she had missed him so very badly.

Deep down she still did. A part of her was missing. There was a hole that no one else could possibly fill. The bond between them had been strong.

When Mrs. Clark lifted her head once more, she stared directly at Halle for so long she feared she had said the wrong thing. She was making a decision, Halle knew, but what would it be?

"Very well," she said slowly but firmly. "I will tell you the story and *you* can find the right words. It's time."

Halle's lips spread into a smile and she nodded. "I would love to."

Silence filled the room for a long minute.

"I was almost forty before the good Lord blessed me with a child."

Halle reached into her bag for her notepad and a pen. "Do you mind if I take notes?"

A glint of bravado flashed in Nancy's gray eyes. "I'd mind if you didn't."

A nervous laugh bubbled up in Halle's throat, and she relaxed. She placed her notepad on the table and flipped to a clean page, then readied her pen.

"Andrew and I were so happy when Andy came into our lives," Nancy said, her voice soft, her gaze lost to some faraway time and place. "We wanted to raise our boy somewhere safe, with good schools. We did a great deal of research before selecting Winchester." She sighed. "It was perfect when we found this house right next door to a couple who had a child almost the same age." She stared at Halle for a moment. "Andy adored you."

"I adored him."

Distance filled her gaze once more. "We were happier than we'd ever believed it was possible to be."

"What do you remember about that day, Mrs. Clark?"

It wasn't necessary for Halle to be more specific. The other woman understood what she meant.

"March 1. Wednesday. I walked to school with you and Andy that day. It was chilly, like today." Her lips—lips that hung in a perpetual frown—lifted slightly with a faint smile. "He was wearing that worn-out orange hoodie. He loved that thing but it was so old and shabby. I feared the other children would make fun of him."

"I remember that hoodie. I begged my mother to

get me one just like it but, you know my parents, they're hardcore Alabama football fans. No orange allowed. And don't worry, no one ever made fun of Andy. All the other kids liked him."

Mrs. Clark dabbed at her eyes with her napkin. "Thank you for saying so."

"My dad picked me up early that afternoon," Halle said. "He'd had to take Mother to the hospital."

Nancy nodded. "I remember."

What Halle's mother had thought was a lingering cold turned out to be pneumonia. She'd almost waited too long before admitting that she needed to see a doctor. They'd hospitalized her immediately. Halle had stayed with her Aunt Daisy for a solid week in that garage apartment where she lived now.

But that day, March 1 twenty-five years ago, the police had arrived before supper. Within twenty-four hours reporters from all over the state were camped out on the street.

Andy Clark had vanished.

"I was late," Nancy confessed, pain twisting her face. "Andrew was at work in Tullahoma and I had a flat tire. With your parents at the hospital, there was nothing to do but call someone to repair my tire. By the time I was backing out of the driveway, school had been out for only fifteen minutes but that was fifteen minutes too long."

"According to the police report," Halle said, "witnesses stated that Andy waited about ten minutes and then started to walk home."

She nodded. "There were witnesses who saw him less than a block from home."

Whoever took him had snatched him only a few hundred yards from his own front door.

"There was never a ransom demand," Halle said. "No contact at all from the kidnapper."

"Nothing." A heavy breath shook the woman's frail shoulders. "It was as if he disappeared into thin air."

"You and your husband hired private investigators." Halle's parents had said as much.

"The police and our community searched for weeks. But there was nothing. Not the hoodie. Not his backpack. Nothing. No other witnesses ever came forward."

These were all details Halle already knew. But perhaps there would be others she didn't. Something that no one knew. There was one thing she would very much like to know. She hoped the question wouldn't put Mrs. Clark off.

"I would like to ask you one question before we go any further."

The lady held her gaze, a surprising courage in her expression. "I'm listening."

"What made you decide to grant an interview now? To me?"

The courage vanished and that dark hollowness was back.

Halle immediately regretted having asked the

question. When she was about to open her mouth to apologize, Mrs. Clark spoke.

"I'm dying. I have perhaps two or three months. It's time the world knew the whole story. If anyone tells it, it should be you."

A chill rushed over Halle's skin. "I will do all within my power to tell the story the way you want it told."

"I'm counting on you, Halle. I want the *whole* story told the right way."

Halle nodded slowly, though she wasn't entirely clear what the older woman meant by the *whole* story. But she fully intended to find out.

Whatever had happened to Andy, the world needed to know.

Halle needed to know.

THEN

Wednesday, March 1
Twenty-five years ago...

HALLE HATED HER pink jacket.

Pink was for scaredy-cat girls. She was a girl but she was no scaredy-cat.

She was a brave, strong kid like Andy.

She wanted an orange hoodie like the one he wore.

"Wear this jacket today," her mom said with a big sigh, "and I will get you an orange one."

Halle made a face. She might only be seven but she wasn't sure if her mommy was telling her the truth or if she was just too tired to argue.

"Promise?"

Judith smiled and offered her little finger. "Pinkie promise."

Halle curled her pinkie around her mommy's. "Okay."

"Come along," Mommy urged. "Andy and his mom are waiting."

At the door her mommy gave her a kiss and waved as Halle skipped out to the sidewalk where Andy and his mom stood.

He had on that orange hoodie and Halle hoped her mommy was really going to get her one.

"Hey," Halle said.

Andy tipped his head back the tiniest bit. "Hey."

He had the bluest eyes of any kid in school. Halle wondered how it was possible to have eyes that blue. Bluer than the sky even.

"How are you this morning, Halle?" Mrs. Clark asked.

"I'm good but my mommy's still a little sick." Halle didn't like when her mommy or daddy was sick. It made her tummy ache.

"I'm sure she'll be better soon," Mrs. Clark assured her. "That pink jacket looks awfully pretty with your red hair."

Halle grimaced. "Thank you but I don't like it

very much." She gazed longingly at Andy's orange hoodie.

He took her hand. "Come on. We're gonna be late."

Halle smiled. He was the best friend ever. They were going to be friends forever and ever.

They walked along, swinging their clasped hands and singing that silly song they'd made up during winter break.

We're gonna sail on a ship...
We're gonna fly on a plane...
We're gonna take that train...
We're taking a trip...

But Andy wasn't supposed to go without her.

Chapter Two

NOW

Wednesday, March 11
Napa, California

"This one is addressed to you personally."

Liam glanced up from the monthly reports he'd been poring over. "What was that?"

His assistant peered over her reading glasses. "Please tell me that's a dating site you're focused on, because if it's work, I'm going to be very upset. This is supposed to be a day off for you. You've been working seven days a week for months now. You need a life, Liam Hart! And I need at least one after-noon to try organizing this…clutter." She surveyed the stacks and piles of binders and folders around his office. "You need someone to do your filing."

Liam closed his laptop before she dared to come around behind him and peek at his screen. "I like my filing system," he pointed out. "You know as well as I do that a little extra time in the fields goes with the territory after a particularly wet season. All that rain calls for extra attention. We both know there's always plenty to do in preparation for—"

She gave him a look that stopped him midsentence. Shelly Montrose had kicked aside the idea of retiring at sixty-five, over two years ago. She had worked for this vineyard for most of her life, first as a picker when she was a child, right after the operation was started by the Josephson family. Then as his father's and now his personal assistant for the past twenty odd years. She was in charge and no one was going to tell her differently.

Certainly not Liam. She knew as much about running this place as he did. Probably more.

"Claire said," he offered in his most amenable tone, since the last thing in the world he wanted to do was upset his favorite lady, "there were reports I needed to see, so I only came by for a couple of hours and then I'm off. I promise."

Claire was his younger sister. At only twenty-five she'd already finished college and had proven herself as a master winemaker. She would say that their continued success since their father's passing was as much Liam's hard work as her own, but that wasn't entirely true. Yes, he was out there in the fields working alongside his crew through the process of winemaking, from tending the plants to bottling. But it was Claire who had the creative vision in developing unique blends and tastes that had put them on the map over the past two years. Their father would be proud.

"Claire." Shelly huffed a breath. "That girl is as bad as you are. She's never going to find a husband if she doesn't stay out of this vineyard! Your daddy took time to raise the two of you and the vineyard didn't go to pot. Your mother is traveling all over Europe and she has repeatedly invited the two of you to join her. Now would be the perfect time for a nice vacation."

"You're right, Shelly." Liam stood and gave her his best smile. "I'm heading out for lunch with a friend right now. The monthly reports be damned."

Her eyes rounded. "A female friend?"

"Yes, ma'am." He reached for his cap and tugged it on. "She's a pretty, blue-eyed girl."

Shelly rolled her eyes and extended the envelope toward him. "Your sister doesn't count."

Liam accepted the letter, tucked it into the hip pocket of his jeans and started around his desk. "I won't tell her you said that."

He left the office and walked through the winery. He loved this place. The rustic beams overhead, the decades-old barrels used for aging. The cobblestone floor. This was his life. Deep down he wouldn't mind having someone to share it with, but that hadn't happened so far. Maybe it was his fault for being so focused on work. But he loved his job.

He couldn't imagine not doing exactly what he did every day.

Outside, the stunning valley view never ceased to make him pause to take it all in. The trees and the pond, all of it gave him a feeling of home. He'd lived right here on this former chicken farm for as far back as he could remember. His father bought the place from the previous owners who had lost interest in trying to jump-start the business after several years of hard times. Over the decades his father had renovated the place into one of sheer beauty and productivity. The vineyards were gorgeous. But they had never been able to compete with the top winemakers when it came to the wines they created.

Liam's father had been good, damned good, but not nearly as good as Claire. She was one of a kind. A rare vintner with a special touch.

He climbed into his truck and slid behind the steering wheel. The crinkling of the envelope in his back pocket reminded him that he had mail. He started the truck and reached for the envelope.

As Shelly had said, it wasn't addressed to the Hart Family Vineyards, but to him. Liam Hart.

No return address on the front or on the back. He frowned, lifted the flap enough to slide his thumb beneath it and to tear it open. Inside was a newspaper, or, at least, part of one. The front page, to be precise. He unfolded the single page and first noted the name of the paper, *Winchester Gazette*,

Winchester, Tennessee. Then he scanned the bold headline at the top of the page.

The Lost Boy—25 Years Later.

His frown deepened. Why would anyone send him a newspaper clipping from Winchester, Tennessee? He checked the postmark. Yep, definitely from Winchester.

To his knowledge he didn't know anyone in the area. He searched his memory. There was, if he recalled correctly, a winery near Winchester. Though not one he'd ever visited. Rather than beat his head against a brick wall trying to remember, he started to read.

Seven-year-old Andy Clark disappeared on March 1, twenty-five years ago. To date there have been no remains found. No further witnesses came forward with reports of having seen the child. He left school, walking, and was nearly home when he vanished, never to be heard from again.

The article went on about the boy and his devastated family and the endless search.

Liam's gut tightened. He avoided stories like this. Every time he heard about a missing child on the news, he felt sick. A natural reaction, he supposed. Who wouldn't get sick at the idea? What kind of person stole a child?

He started to fold the paper and toss it aside, but

his gaze landed on the series of photos included with the article.

The beating in his chest lost a step, then suddenly burst into hyper speed.

The photos of the little boy were…

Him.

Not just the chubby-cheeked image of any child, but his particular features, his smile, his eyes, his… attitude.

"No way," he muttered, his face pinched as he stared at the images.

Okay, this was bizarre. Shaking his head at his foolishness, he backed out of the parking slot and drove across the property, past the pond and the visitors' deck, to the private residence. Both he and his sister lived in the house. She had the wing that had once been the guest suite while he slept in the room he'd had for as long as he could remember. Suited him just fine. Though he had stored away the sports trophies and award certificates from school. His space was more of a bachelor pad.

A bachelor who still lived in the house where he'd grown up.

"Nothing wrong with that," he said to his reflection in the rearview mirror.

The newspaper clipping clasped tightly, he climbed out of the truck and walked to the house. He entered the key code and opened the door.

His heart still raced as he strode across the entry hall and toward the family room. His mother had all the family photo albums lined up on shelves. She loved nothing more than showing off her kids. She was actually Liam's stepmother; his biological mom had died when he was a baby. But Penelope Hart had treated him as much like her own as she had Claire—whom she'd given birth to.

If Penelope were here she would get a kick out of the photos in the newspaper article. He managed a smile at the thought but still...this felt weird. Particularly since someone on the other side of the country had mailed it to him. As far as he knew, he had no friends, relatives or even acquaintances in the area.

This was obviously someone's idea of a joke.

He spread the newspaper's front page on the coffee table, then strode to the bookcases built along the wall adjacent to the fireplace. Penelope had carefully dated each album. Finding the one for the proper time frame was easy. He carried the album to the coffee table and sat down on the edge of the couch.

His breath caught in his throat. The resemblance between him and the missing boy was uncanny. Completely bizarre. He removed two photos from the album and placed them next to the images in the newspaper.

"Holy..." Looking at the photos side by side triggered a strong emotion he couldn't label, which sank deep into his bones.

There had to be an explanation. Maybe he'd been a twin and his parents hadn't known. The missing child could have been his twin brother. His father

had told him that he and his mother had been homeless when he was born. Living in the hills and woods
of northern California like a couple of disenfran-
chised hippies. Who knew what sort of prenatal care
she received?

It was possible that there had been two babies.

He moved his head side to side. Even as shaken as
he was at the moment, he recognized he was reach-
ing with that scenario.

Leaving the disturbing newspaper where it lay,
he walked out of the family room and along the
corridor until he came to the office that had been
his father's—the office that was his now. He hit the
switch, turning on the lights. The closet had been
turned into a built-in safe. Using the dial, he quickly
went through the combination steps, lifted the lever
and opened it. He located the file with birth certificates and withdrew his. His fingers roamed over the
state seal as he considered the information printed
on the document. Nothing unusual or unexpected
there. Closing the safe, he moved to one of the many
file cabinets and looked through the folders until he
found the one with his name. Inside was his school
vaccination record. His academic reports.

He flipped through page after page.

It was all there. From kindergarten through senior
year and then his acceptance papers for the Univer-
sity of California.

What was he doing?

He closed the filing drawer and walked out, turning off the lights as he went. Whoever sent the paper to him had accomplished his mission. The joke was on Liam.

As he left the house, he grabbed the newspaper and the photos of him as a kid. He had to show this to Claire.

His sister was a hell of a mystery buff. Maybe someone would get a laugh out of this.

Angele Restaurant

"I THOUGHT I'd been stood up," Claire chided as he pulled out a chair at her table.

"Sorry, there was something I had to do." He reached for his water glass and considered ordering a shot of bourbon. Sweat had beaded on his forehead during the drive here.

It was ridiculous. Heart palpitations and sweating? He was a little freaked out. He had to get a grip.

Maybe Shelly was right. He had been working too hard. He needed a break.

"I've already ordered for the both of us. Roasted chicken salad." She placed one hand atop the other on the table and studied him. "What's wrong? You look—" she shrugged "—strangely unsettled."

His sister had Penelope's eyes. Blue but a light blue, almost gray. Her hair was a darker blond than his, as well, more brown than blond. But the high cheekbones and the Roman nose, she'd gotten both those from their father, just as Liam had.

He pulled the folded newspaper and the two photos from the family album out of his hip pocket and placed them on the table. "Someone mailed this newspaper page to me. No name or return address. Just the front page of this small-town newspaper." He tapped the now wrinkled page.

While Claire read, Liam surveyed the restaurant. He'd been here a hundred times at least. The rustic French decor was not unlike their home, which Penelope and his father had turned into a classic yet rustic French château. It was warm and relaxing, much like this restaurant. And the food here was the best in Napa. He had yet to order a single dish that was anything less than incredible.

Claire placed the newspaper on the table, folded so that the photos of the boy—Andy Clark—were prominent. Then she laid the two photos of Liam next to them.

"Holy moly," she whispered. "This is...this is totally cray cray."

Crazy. Definitely.

"There was no name on the envelope?" she asked though he'd already told her as much.

He shook his head. "No name. No address. But the envelope is postmarked Winchester, Tennessee."

She stared at the paper again. "Have you ever been to this place?"

"Never."

"Well." She refolded the paper and tucked the

loose photos inside the fold before passing the tidy bundle to him. "Someone thinks you have."

He made a sound he'd intended as a laugh, but it came out more like a choking noise. "What does that mean?"

"It means that whoever sent you this newspaper clipping believes you are this boy."

This notion had been festering in the back of his brain since he opened the damned envelope but he had refused to allow it to fully reach the surface.

"That's insane." He shook his head. "How would this person even know who I am or where I live?"

"I don't know." Claire's brow lined the way it did when she was stumped by some issue with a new blend she'd created.

"Hey," he argued, "come on. We grew up together. You know this is impossible as well as ridiculous."

She stared at him, unblinking, unflinching. "You were almost eight when I was born. We grew up together after that point." She glanced at the bundled paper lying next to his water glass.

"Now you're just being a —"

"No," she countered, "think about it. This could be real, Liam. Go back to the house and look at the family photo albums again. Try to find any of yourself—at least any in which you can see your face—between being a little baby and seven or eight years old."

"What?" Now he got it. She had done this. As

a prank. Yes, that had to be it. She wanted him to work for the payoff, sending him on a wild-goose chase. "You did this because of what I did on your birthday." He shook his head, felt a sudden rush of relief. "I told you I was sorry. You didn't have to go to this extreme."

When she'd turned twenty-five, he'd put one of those happy birthday ads in the *Napa Valley Register* announcing that Claire was actually thirty. She had not thought it was funny. She had warned that she would get even with him.

He laughed. Laughed long and hard, almost lost his breath as waves of giddy relief washed over him.

When he'd finished, the people at several tables were staring at them.

"You finished?" she demanded, one eyebrow hiked up.

He held up his hands. "You got me, sis. I have to tell you, I was freaking out."

"I didn't do this, Liam." Her tone was flat and serious.

That chill he'd been fighting since he'd opened that damned envelope seeped into his bones anew.

"Okay." He suddenly wished he hadn't told her. Maybe she didn't have some fake newspaper printed and mailed to him from Winchester, Tennessee, but she was sure taking advantage of the opportunity.

"I even asked Mom once."

Enough. And yet, he couldn't not take the bait. "Asked her what?"

"Why there were no pictures of you during kindergarten or when you were three or four. There are hundreds of me, but there's this big gap in your documented history. I thought it was strange."

"I can honestly say I've never noticed." Why the hell didn't the food arrive? Anything to change the subject. Now he didn't want to talk about it.

"Of course you haven't. That's a girl thing. The women maintain the family photos and store keepsakes. Most guys don't even notice."

"What did she say?" He really wanted this discussion to end. He should have taken the day off like Shelly said.

"She said the photos and stuff for that time period were lost in a fire."

"There you go." He shrugged, felt some measure of relief once more. "That explains it."

"No, that doesn't explain anything. Because I asked Joe about the fire and he had no idea what I was talking about."

"Joe Brown?" Liam held up his hands. "Claire, Joe died when you were thirteen."

Joe had been the vineyard manager when Liam was growing up. In truth he'd been like an uncle to both him and Claire.

"I asked about the photos when I was twelve. Remember that school project I had to do using family photos? It was that ancestry thing."

He shrugged again, his frustration building far too rapidly. "Not really."

"I'm telling you that I asked Mother and she made up a story about a fire in the family room. When I mentioned the fire to Joe, he said there was never a fire in the house. Never, Liam."

"I'm not talking about this anymore." He didn't know what he'd expected Claire to say when he'd shown her the clipping and photos, but once he'd latched on to the prank theory, he'd realized how much he wanted that to be true. Not this…this other possibility.

Thankfully, the food arrived, saving him from having to argue further with Claire. He should have known better than to tell her about this.

When the waiter had moved on, Liam dug in. He hadn't realized until that moment that he was starving. Hopefully, Claire would take his cue and eat instead of pursuing this ridiculous idea.

Unfortunately, the silence didn't last long.

"We should call Mom."

"For the love of God, Claire." He put his fork down and braced his palms on the table. "I don't want to talk about this anymore. The whole notion is ludicrous. I shouldn't have shown you the article."

She reached across the table and snatched up the newspaper, opened it enough to find whatever she was looking for. She tapped the byline beneath the headline. "You need to call this Halle Lane. Maybe she sent the newspaper to you."

When he didn't respond, she went further.

"Maybe you should do better than call," she said. "Maybe go to Winchester. Check this out in person."

He looked at her as if she'd suggested he go to the moon. He now regretted even reading the article, let alone sharing it with her.

"I think you should." She gave him a nod. "Maybe the visit will trigger a memory of living there."

He rolled his eyes. "The only thing I remember about being seven is a bicycle accident that gave me a broken arm and a concussion."

It was the worst memory of his childhood.

But it was real, and his father had been right there with him through the whole thing.

THEN

Twenty-five years ago...

"I'M SCARED AND my head hurts bad. My arm, too."

His father's arms tightened around him, pulling him closer to his chest—close enough that he could feel his heart pounding. His father was scared, too.

"You're going to be fine, son. The doctor says you have a mild concussion. I promise you'll be better in a few days."

He closed his eyes tighter and tried to remember why he was so scared. He remembered the headlights coming at him. He remembered falling. For a moment he'd thought he was dead.

Then his father had been there telling him he was okay. Calling an ambulance.

He remembered drifting in and out. He wanted to stay awake but it was so hard. He couldn't keep his eyes open and going to sleep made the pain go away.

His father wouldn't let him sleep. He'd wake him up each time he drifted off.

"Stay with me now."

Lights pulsed in the darkness. Made his head hurt worse. He wanted to go home. He was cold. So cold. His head hurt so bad. And his arm. He couldn't move it without the pain making him cry harder.

Two men in uniforms suddenly hovered over him in his memory or the dream he was having. It was hard to tell which. They kept telling him he would be okay. They were taking him to the hospital. He would get to ride in the ambulance.

But he didn't want to go to the hospital.

He wanted to go home.

Why couldn't he just go home?

He felt his body being moved. Lifted onto a stretcher and then they rolled him to the ambulance.

His father climbed in with him, sat close to him, kept telling him he would be fine.

He only wanted to close his eyes and pretend this didn't happen. He didn't want to be in an ambulance. He didn't want his head and arm to hurt so bad.

He wanted to go home.

The ambulance was moving now and he suddenly felt the urge to throw up. He struggled to hold it back. Didn't want to throw up in front of these strangers.

He felt weird. Like he was here, except not.

He just wanted to go home.

Tears slid down his face. He felt them slip into his ears. His head and arm hurt too much to bother trying to wipe them away.

He felt hands on his face, wiping away his tears. His father leaned close, his lips to his forehead. "Shhh, don't cry, sweet Liam. Everything will be fine. *You* will be fine."

He realized then why he was so afraid.

Who was Liam?

Chapter Three

Thursday, March 12
Winchester, Tennessee

Halle had beamed all week. Today was no exception. Lunch with Audrey, her boss, had proven she had every right to be excited. The entire staff at the paper was immensely proud of her, even Rog.

Her story on the lost boy had been picked up through wire services in some of the largest markets in the country. Reporters had flocked to Winchester. One of the biggest network morning shows had asked to interview her.

She had done it. She'd made her comeback as a journalist.

A grin slid across her face. And her old friend Andy Clark had helped her. This was the story she had needed to get her career back on track. It had been right under her nose all along.

She'd spent the afternoon walking on clouds but now it was time to get to work. Reality had slammed into her at about four. It was five thirty now. Most of the staff had gone home. Only Tanya, the receptionist downstairs in the lobby, and Brian, the editor, were still in the main office. Halle was fairly certain Brian never went home. He probably had a cot in the basement. As for Tanya, Halle was equally certain she had a thing for Brian and hung around just to be near him.

Audrey wanted Halle to focus solely on this case. They'd been swamped with tips since the story ran, everything from alien abduction suggestions to complicated tales of crime rings. Audrey wanted her to find the rest of the story. What really happened to Andy Clark? Mrs. Clark had said she would be happy to talk to Halle more.

If the police and the FBI hadn't been able to figure it out, how in the world was she supposed to do it?

She wanted to, certainly. She would have her choice of any assignment in the country if she managed to dig up that whole story.

But the idea was a little off the charts.

Halle moistened her lips, ordered her heart to slow its damned galloping.

Maybe she could do this. Audrey had given her full access to any necessary resources. She'd even offered to introduce her to Luther Holcomb, the chief of police at the time of Andy's disappearance. Holcomb was a bit of a hermit nowadays but Audrey's husband, Sheriff Colt Tanner, knew the man personally.

Before she did anything else, she needed to see Mrs. Clark again. The older woman had gotten a headache and had to lie down the last time they spoke about Andy. On Sunday afternoon, she had gone to her house again and taken her two copies of the newspaper. She'd reiterated then that perhaps they could make the articles a series. Get deeper into the story of before and after Andy. Mrs. Clark had actually sounded excited about the possibility.

What Audrey had asked Halle to do was different. Her vision was about finding the whole story, to do what the police and detectives hadn't been able to do—discover what really happened to Andy. Mrs. Clark had said she wanted the entire tale told. Maybe she should start by asking where would Andy be now if he was alive? Where did he go that day and who took him? What parent wouldn't want to know what really happened to their child?

It was worth a shot. She cringed as she thought of resurrecting Mrs. Clark's pain. Reporters weren't supposed to have soft hearts. Being ruthless and relentless was more than a little important to get to the truth.

Still, this was different. This was Andy and Andy's mother.

Mrs. Clark had okayed pursuing the story so far. If Halle had misunderstood the woman's intent, she would have to back off. She didn't really want to go down this path without her blessing. It felt wrong.

She wouldn't use Andy or his mother just to advance her career. If she continued with the story it would be because she wanted the truth as much as Mrs. Clark did. She stared at the stack of messages on her desk. Networks and newspapers from across the country wanted to talk to her.

She could do this even if Mrs. Clark changed her mind after all the notoriety—as long as she was careful not to cause pain for the woman. Of course she would never do such a thing. Mrs. Clark and her husband had been victims of the worst kind of crime. They didn't deserve to be hurt any further. Halle couldn't be the reason for that.

She wouldn't be.

Her cell rang and she checked the screen. *Mom*.

"Hey, Mom." She almost added that yes, she would be home for dinner since that was likely the reason for the call.

"Hey, sweetie. Just wanted to warn you that the reporters have already started to camp on the sidewalk."

The crew had been here in the parking lot all day every day this week. They had figured out her schedule, particularly when she headed home. So far, a deputy had escorted Halle to her car each evening. But she hadn't called for an escort today. The reporters had figured out her MO. Now they waited for her at home.

She couldn't hold it against them. She would do and had done the same thing.

"Do you and Dad want to meet me for dinner somewhere?"

"No, that's not necessary. I've already started dinner. Your favorite, lasagna. I just wanted to be sure you would be here and to warn you about the vultures out front."

Halle laughed. "I'm one of those vultures, Mom."

The whisper of her chuckle reached across the line. "I'm sure you're always thoughtful and considerate when going after a story."

"Of course," Halle fibbed as she remembered times when she'd had to be aggressive to get to a reluctant source. "You and Dad raised me that way."

"So you'll be here? Maybe you can park on the street behind us and sneak in again so they won't bother you. Or I could have Daddy sit on the porch with his shotgun."

The idea made Halle smile in spite of herself. "No, Mom, that's not necessary. I'll be fine. I'll be home around six or so."

"All right, sweetie. Love you."

"Love you, too."

Halle ended the call and stared at her cell for a moment. Her parents had raised her to be kind. Though she had always been relentless going after the story, she did try to be considerate—most of the time.

She pulled open her middle drawer and picked up the photo she'd brought to the office as inspiration while she wrote the article on the lost boy. It was a picture of her with Andy the fall before he went missing. They were at the school Halloween carnival. She had been dressed as a fairy with wings and all. He'd been Batman, complete with the cape and mask. Their faces were jammed cheek to cheek for the shot. She couldn't recall which mother snapped the pic, hers or his.

There were so many fun times like this one. She'd spent the first year after he was lost in a state of depression. Her parents had tried every way to cheer her up but nothing had worked. Finally, she had moved on to some degree. By the time she was ten she had stopped being so sad but she still missed him.

But she had always wondered what if. What if he hadn't disappeared? What if they had grown up together? Would they still be friends? Would it have turned into more? They had pretended to get married once. A smile tugged at her lips. She and her parents had attended the wedding of the daughter of a friend of her mother's. Halle had been so enthralled by the decorated church and the wedding dress she had rushed home afterward and told Andy they had to get married.

He'd shrugged and said okay. He'd always been up for whatever made her happy.

Funny, maybe that was why she'd never found the right guy. Maybe the right guy had disappeared twenty-five years ago.

"I'm sorry, Halle."

She looked up as Tanya burst into the room.

"I tried to tell him we were closed. I was locking up when he bullied his way through the door."

A tall man stood in the corridor beyond Tanya. She watched his nervous movements through the open door. He was looking side to side as if he feared security would be showing up any second.

"He says he needs to speak with you about the article."

She sighed. "Is he a reporter?"

"No. He said he has some information, though. And some questions."

They'd had a lot of emails with "clues" since the article ran, nearly all of them crazy, some asking if there was reward money, many mentioning children who looked like the photos of Andy, as if he would still be seven years old. She wasn't up to talking to one of those tipsters face-to-face.

Tanya went on, "He says he has some pictures."

A shiver ran up Halle's spine. Maybe she'd talk to this one, just this one, and get him out of the way so Tanya could go home.

"It's all right, Tanya." Halle stood. "I'll talk to him."

Tanya nodded and turned to go. The man stepped out of her way and she hurried off down the corridor.

That was the moment Halle got her first full glimpse of the unexpected visitor as he stepped into her office doorway.

Tall, blond. Very good-looking.

His gaze collided with hers.

Blue eyes. The bluest she had ever seen.

Her heart stumbled. Tension rifled through her, and her face flushed, her muscles clenched.

"How…" She cleared her throat of the strange emotion lodged there. "How can I help you?"

He held out a wrinkled page from a newspaper. "Are you Halle Lane?"

She nodded, still grappling for composure. Who was this man? "Yes."

He stepped fully into her office, still holding out the newspaper as if it were a weapon or something otherwise lethal. The thought chilled her. Why had she said she'd see him? "Did you write this article?"

She extended her arm across her desk. He shoved the newspaper close enough for her to take it from him without touching his fingers or his hand. It was the front page of Sunday's paper, the one with her article on Andy's disappearance.

"Yes. I did."

His jaw tightened. "Did you mail that to me?" he snapped.

She blinked. "What? No. I don't even know your name, sir. How could I mail anything to you?"

He had no discernible accent. His skin was tanned. He wore jeans and a tee. The tee sported the logo from a Napa Valley vineyard. Surely he hadn't come all the way from California to talk to her. If he had...

The curiosity she'd experienced earlier morphed into fear. Maybe this was a mistake. She suddenly wished Tanya had called 911 and wondered if she could surreptitiously dial it on her cell.

Something was very, very wrong.

Rather than respond to her question, he stood there, staring at her as if he'd suddenly lost his ability to speak. Frankly, he looked shell-shocked. Halle wasn't sure whether she should call for medical assistance or the police.

"Are you okay?" she asked, then decided calming him was the best course of action. "Why don't we begin again?" she suggested "Please, have a seat. I'm sure we can sort this out."

Somehow he found his way into the chair in front of her desk without taking his eyes off her face.

Halle settled into her chair. "You know who I am. May I ask your name?"

"Liam." He swallowed hard. "Liam Hart."

Summoning a polite smile, she gave him a nod. "Mr. Hart, why don't you tell me what happened? You mentioned someone mailed my article to you?"

His head moved up and down, slowly. "Yesterday. It was addressed to me at my office in...in California."

"You came all the way from California to ask me

about the article?" She tried not to allow the tension to slip into her voice again.

He looked away. "I'm not some stalker or crazy person." His gaze met hers once more. "I came because…"

Rather than finish his sentence he reached into the pocket of his tee and withdrew something, tossed the items on her desk. Photographs. She grabbed them, her pulse racing toward some unseen finish line for reasons still unknown to her.

"I came because of the photos that accompanied your article."

Halle stared at the two photos. *Andy.* "Where did you get these?" she practically whispered.

For a moment he only continued to stare at her.

Who was this man? How did he have these photos of Andy? Why were his eyes so blue?

The idea that he might be… No, no, it wasn't possible.

Was it?

"Those photos came from a family album," he finally said. "My family album."

She left the photos on her desk and clasped her hands together to conceal their shaking. "Do you…" She moistened her lips, tried to swallow, but it wasn't happening. "Do you know the boy in these photos?"

The question was foolish. The photos had been in his family's album. Of course he knew who the boy was.

"Me."

The single syllable quaked through her. Not possible. "I'm not sure I understand." She held up one of the photos. "I know this boy. His name is Andrew—Andy Clark. He went missing twenty-five years ago."

Mr. Hart shook his head. "Those photos are me. That house you see in the background is my home. In California."

Halle stared at the photo with the house. It certainly wasn't a house in her neighborhood. Definitely not Andy's house.

"The dog in the other one," he said, "that's Sparky. The dog my father got me for my birthday."

Halle's head was spinning. This was incomprehensible. She struggled for rational thought, for what to do next. "Mr. Hart, I can't explain why you look exactly like Andy." She simultaneously shook her head and shrugged awkwardly. "I honestly don't know what to say. I can see why you were shaken by the article and the photos. If the photos you brought with you are of you—" she tapped the newspaper "—and I know these are of Andy…" She looked him in the eyes. "Let me pursue this. With you. We could both work on it. In ways that law enforcement can't."

The reporter in her wouldn't allow the opportunity to pass without trying to get to the truth.

LIAM STARED at the woman. He'd been doing that practically from the moment he laid eyes on her. She seemed so familiar to him. Like someone he'd gone to school with or met at a party. Somehow he knew this Halle Lane. From the wild mane of red hair to the freckles and those too familiar green eyes.

"I came here to ask you," he said, his chest heavy with some emotion he couldn't define, "about this Andy—the boy who went missing. I tried to google for information but what I found was vague at best. There was no explanation of what happened to him."

"I can tell you anything you want to know," she assured him. "Andy and I were neighbors and best friends. But, to my knowledge, no one knows what happened to him. The police, the FBI, even private investigators were never able to solve the case."

Best friends. Neighbors. Liam drew in a big breath. "All right." He glanced around her office. "My flight got into Nashville and I drove straight here. I don't have a hotel yet, but maybe we should have dinner. Talk. I'll find a place to stay later."

He felt like a total idiot. Talk? Dinner? But then, he was here. He'd come a long way to get some answers. He might as well get those answers straight from the horse's mouth, so to speak.

"There's a couple of options for lodging," she said. "As you say, we can worry about that later. I don't know about you but I'm starving. My parents are expecting me for dinner. Why don't you join us?"

He blinked, startled at the invitation. "Sure. If you think your parents won't mind."

She laughed. "I can guarantee you they won't mind. And a dinner out might draw attention you don't want or need."

He grabbed his photos from her desk and tucked them back into his pocket. "I can follow you."

"Actually—" she picked up her shoulder bag "—it would be better if we rode together. We'll have to park on another street and sneak into my backyard. Reporters are camping out in front of my house."

He wasn't so sure that being without his own transportation was a good idea.

"Don't worry," she offered, "I'll bring you back for your car."

Too tired to argue and too curious to miss out on the opportunity, he said, "Fine."

Fine might be an overstatement but he would ride it out.

The dreams that had haunted him last night wouldn't fade. As a boy, he hadn't been able to remember his name at the ER when he'd broken his arm. The doctor had assured his father that it was probably the concussion causing the confusion and it would likely clear up in a couple of days. And it had.

Maybe the newspaper article wouldn't have gotten to him if it hadn't been for that one disturbing memory in that hospital…and Claire's insistence that there were no pictures of him.

He was here. He intended to find out what his true past was.

SHE PARKED ON a short, shady street that wasn't so different from some of the streets back home. Liam surveyed the neat yards and the quaint old houses.

He reached into the back seat and got his jacket. He'd almost left it in his rental. The temperature had dropped dramatically after sunset. Something else that reminded him of home.

"This way," she said in a stage whisper.

He followed her between two houses and across the backyard of the one on the right. No exterior lights came on, no dogs barked. The moon and the glow from the windows provided just enough illumination for their trek across the property. A clothesline and a swing set were the only items they encountered.

"Mrs. Jolly is the neighbor who lives behind us," Halle said in a low voice. "I warned her on Monday that I might have to use her backyard to avoid the reporters."

Liam glanced at the back of the small house. He spotted an older woman peering from one of the windows. The light behind her highlighting her presence.

"Here we go."

His guide stopped at a white picket fence and opened the gate. Once they were through, she closed it behind them.

"Home sweet home."

She marched to the back porch and climbed the steps, chattering the whole time about how good her mother's lasagna was and how excited she would be to have a guest for dinner.

The overhead light came on and the door opened

as they crossed the porch. An older version of the woman he'd followed through the darkness stood in the doorway. Her red hair was shot through with gray and pulled back in a long braid.

"I was beginning to think you weren't coming."

"I was held up at the office. Mom, this is Liam Hart. He's joining us for dinner. Liam—" she glanced at him "—this is my mom, Judith."

"I hope that's okay, ma'am," he said when the mother stared openmouthed at him.

"Yes, of course." She blinked once, twice. "Come in."

As they entered the house, Judith called out, "Howard! Halle's home and she brought a guest."

The kitchen smelled of garlic and fresh baked bread. Liam watched as the two women chatted excitedly—as if he was some celebrity or something. A tall, gray-haired man entered the room.

He hesitated, assessed Liam, then thrust out his right hand. "I'm Howard, the father."

"Liam," he said as he shook the man's hand. "Liam Hart."

"Let's eat before it gets cold," Judith announced.

They gathered around the table that stood on one end of the massive kitchen. The whole back of the house appeared to be a kitchen. It was nice. Homey. Looked well loved. That was one of the things he liked most about his family home. It was a real home. Used and loved and…his. His home. Whatever happened here twenty-five years ago had nothing to do with him. Whoever mailed that newspaper to him had made a mistake.

"So, Liam," Howard said as the various dishes made the rounds of those seated at the table, "tell us about you."

"I'm from Napa. My sister and I run the Hart Family Winery. It's been in my family for more than two decades."

"Oh, my," Judith said. "Would you prefer wine rather than the sweet iced tea?"

"No, ma'am. The tea is fine."

"Sweetheart," Howard announced, "I do believe you've outdone yourself. The lasagna is splendid."

Liam ignored his salad and took a bite of the lasagna. Halle's father was right. It was exceptional. He smiled at Judith. "Really outstanding."

She beamed at him. Something deep inside him shifted. He looked from Judith to Howard and then to Halle. These people shouldn't feel so damned familiar to him.

This was all wrong.

THEN

Monday, October 31
Twenty-five years, five months ago...

HALLE DIDN'T WANT to be a fairy. She wanted to be Robin. Andy was Batman and she wanted to be

Robin. They were best friends after all. Just like Batman and Robin.

Their moms walked behind them, not allowing them to get too far ahead. Even though they knew everyone on this street and all the other streets around them, their moms always worried.

"I like your costume," Andy said.

Halle smiled at him. "Like yours, too. I wanted to be Robin."

They walked on, heading for the next house.

When they turned up the sidewalk, Andy leaned close and whispered, "You are Robin. You're just in disguise. Sometimes superheroes do that."

A big old grin spread across her face. "Yeah. I am Robin. In disguise."

They rushed to the front door and rang the bell. It was her turn, so she was the one to press the lit button.

When the door opened they shouted, "Trick or treat!"

Mr. Olson made a surprised face. "My goodness, I had no idea Batman was in the neighborhood. Who's your friend, Batman?" Mr. Olson winked at Halle.

"It's my friend Robin—in disguise."

"Well, this really is a special visit." He held out the bowl. "Robin, you and Batman take all the treats you want."

Giggling, they grabbed a handful of candy each and dropped it into their pumpkin-head pails.

"Thank you!" they recited simultaneously before dashing away.

"Be careful out there, Batman and Robin," Mr. Olson called after them.

The mothers waited on the sidewalk by the street. Halle and Andy hurried past and headed for the next house.

"Thanks for letting me be Robin even in this fairy suit," Halle said as they skipped up the sidewalk to the next house.

"You'll always be my Robin," Andy promised.

"Forever and ever," Halle said on a laugh.

By the time their moms made them go home, they had a ton of candy each. They were never going to run out of candy.

When they reached their end of South High, they parted ways, waving and laughing. It was a good night.

Halle couldn't wait to go to sleep. Tomorrow was a school day. She and Andy were going to trade sandwiches at lunch. On Tuesdays they always did. Halle loved his mom's pastrami sandwiches and he loved her mom's peanut butter and jelly ones.

Maybe she'd sneak some of her Halloween candy in her lunch box to share with Andy.

She couldn't wait until morning.

Chapter Four

NOW

"Dinner was great," Liam said. "Inviting a stranger into your home was very kind of you."

Judith blinked a couple of times. "Oh…of course. Friends of Halle are always welcome."

Liam managed a single nod. But he wasn't a friend. Whatever these people thought, he was a stranger. He had never lived here. He didn't know them or the boy, Andy, who was lost all those years ago. They just happened to resemble each other as children. It happened. No big deal. The question was how had anyone from Winchester found him? Connected him to this old tragedy?

Some reporter—maybe even Halle Lane herself—had likely gone to a great deal of trouble to locate someone who fit the profile of this Andy Clark. Made for great headlines, didn't it?

"I should get a place to stay for the night," he said,

suddenly finding himself completely out of place, out of sorts. "I have a flight back home tomorrow."

Just saying the words made him feel more relaxed. He needed to get back home. To feel grounded.

"So soon?" Halle asked.

"I—I hadn't planned on staying long. Just long enough to…" To what? Now his decision to come all this way seemed silly. What had he hoped to find here? Had he thought he'd be able to tell who sent him the article in a glance, a chance remark? It was a fool's errand, and he was beginning to feel very foolish and uncomfortable.

"Before you go," Halle said quickly, "you can look at my research."

He had flown across the country on a whim because of this mystery. Of course he wanted to see her research. Maybe it would provide a clue to who had sent him the article. "Yes. I'd like that."

"Great." A smile perked up the corners of her mouth.

She had those really nice lips. Full and…

What the hell was he doing?

"Let us know if you need anything while you're here, Liam," Howard offered. "Winchester is a nice town. Lots of friendly people."

"Thank you." Despite their comments, he felt uneasy. Friendly people didn't send articles about a lost child to him with no explanation. Someone in Winchester had done that.

As he wondered again about the sender, Halle

stood, placed their plates in the sink and announced she would take him to see her research before it got too late. He rose, too, and helped clear the rest of the table with her.

"Mom, Dad, good night," Halle said when they were finished.

"Thank you for dinner," Liam added. He smiled for the parents once more, grabbed his jacket and followed Halle out onto the porch. The breeze held a bite. He pulled on his jacket as they descended the steps. "We going back to your office?"

"We're going to my place." She pointed to the detached garage at the end of the long driveway. "I have an apartment over the garage. It's more an office and a place to sleep. I can't even remember the last time I actually watched the television and I've never cooked a meal there."

"Why didn't you stay in Nashville?" He already knew a little about her after he'd done some research on her during the flight today. She'd had a rising career there until things started to go downhill a couple of years ago. She'd been married. No kids.

The internet was full of information about Halle Lane. Not so much about Andy Clark. Most of the information about Liam was related to the winery. There weren't even that many photos of him to be found.

"I made a mistake," she admitted as she started up the stairs on the side of the garage. "I allowed my personal life to invade my professional life. It was a mistake that I paid dearly for."

He mulled over her answer as she paused on the landing to unlock the door. "Sometimes it's difficult to keep things separate."

Running a family-owned and-operated vineyard and winery, he knew from experience that it was next to impossible to keep his personal life from his professional life. They were basically one and the same.

She walked through the door, waited for him to enter, then closed the door. "Sorry about the mess." She gestured to the large open space. "This is the real Halle. Disorganized and perpetually on the run."

An L-shaped sofa sat in the middle of the room. A square coffee table nestled in the vee. Like the coffee table, the sofa was littered with piles of folders and notebooks. On the other side of the sofa was a bay window with a built-in seat. Probably looked out over the backyard. A few feet away was an expanse of cabinetry and small appliances that represented the kitchen. A narrow island was covered with notes and photos. One of the two stools fronting it held yet another stack of folders.

Beyond the kitchen area was a king-size bed— unmade. Its hotel-style white linens lay twisted and crumpled. A door stood on either side of the bed. He figured one was a closet and the other was the bathroom.

"It's larger than I expected," he said. If she ever visited his office she would feel right at home. Shelly was constantly threatening to bring in a bulldozer to clear it out.

She tossed her shoulder bag on the sofa, walked to the loaded stool and began to move the stack of files. "It used to be just storage. But when I was a little girl, my father turned it into an apartment for his younger sister, Daisy." She smiled as she plopped the stack into the window seat. "Daisy was a romance writer. She never told anyone. Only the family knew. She liked having her little secret. No matter that her Lola Renae books were quite popular, she kept her career quiet. Everyone thought she was just the old maid who lived over the Lanes' garage."

"Interesting. My mother loves romance novels." Penelope kept a stack of Harlequins on her bedside table.

"She's probably read a Lola Renae or two."

"I'll have to ask her. She's in Paris right now. Since my dad died, she hasn't spent a lot of time at home. She says she's giving my sister—Claire—and me our space, but I think it's more about not being able to bear the memories now that Dad isn't there."

"Sounds like they had an amazing love story of their own."

He nodded. "They did. Dad said he was totally lost after my biological mom died. She died before I was two. Dad didn't meet Penelope, the only mom

I've ever known, until I was five. They had Claire when I was seven."

Liam had no idea why he'd just told her all those personal things—things that had no bearing on what they had to discuss. Flustered, he slumped onto the stool she'd cleared. She slid onto the other one.

"This is a copy of the case file from the local authorities. Getting a copy from the FBI was not going to happen. Chief of Police Brannigan was kind enough to provide everything he had."

Liam opened the file. Right on top was a photo of the boy, Andy Clark. Again, something in him shuddered. The image shook him. How could the two of them look so much alike?

"That's his school picture from that year. Second grade." A smile tugged at her lips even as her gaze grew distant. "Everyone in the class loved him. The teachers loved him. He was such a sweet kid."

Liam swallowed hard. "He was walking home from school?" Liam had garnered that much from the internet.

"Yes. Usually, we walked together but my dad picked me up that day. Mother was really sick. She'd had to be hospitalized. He picked me up to go see her and then took me home. By then the police were swarming all over our street."

The image of official vehicles parked this way and that on the street flashed through his mind. Dogs barking echoed in his brain.

A shiver coursed through him. "How long did the search go on?"

"For weeks, but each day after the first week, fewer and fewer showed up to participate in the search parties. They checked pools and ponds in the area. Empty houses and buildings. That first week the dogs were involved. Several different police departments from surrounding counties brought their dogs and members of their communities to help in the search. It was a massive undertaking." She exhaled a big breath. "By the first of April, hope had diminished, the same as the search parties."

"You mentioned private investigators." He could imagine that any family with the means would have hired a PI to try to find their missing child.

"The Clarks hired several. No one ever found anything useful."

"Sounds like the kidnapping was a professional job." He couldn't see amateurs getting that lucky.

"Possibly. Or someone who had done this before. A predator."

His gut clenched at the idea. "Sometimes these kids come back, right?"

"Of the hundreds of thousands of children reported missing each year, about ninety-nine percent come back alive. A lot of work is being done to ensure children are found and returned home quickly. But some, like Andy, aren't so lucky."

"So kids like Andy are in the minority."

"That's right. Still, even one percent is too many.

One child is too many. My family and I watched the devastation take a toll on the Clarks. Their life was never the same. When they lost Andy, they lost everything that mattered to them, because with him gone, nothing else was relevant."

"Understandable."

He felt her looking at him. She had questions. He still had questions of his own. The trouble was, neither of them had the right answers.

"Tell me about you, Liam Hart. Besides where you're from and what you do for a living. Tell me about your childhood, your life. Accidents? Surgeries? Illnesses?"

"You want my social security number, too?" The surprise on her face made him smile. "Just kidding."

She put a hand to her throat. "Sorry. I know I can be a little pushy sometimes."

"Sometimes," he agreed. "To answer your many questions, other than the one time I had to be taken to the ER as a kid, I've never been hospitalized. Never been sick really. I guess I was lucky that way. My childhood was uneventful beyond the fact that my sister and I roamed the vineyards. Our parents were always worried we'd hurt ourselves. I thought I had to take Claire everywhere with me. Dad said sometimes he thought I was terrified of losing her." Liam shrugged. "Maybe I was. I didn't like it when she was out of my sight."

Saying those words now seemed wrong somehow. Why would he have been afraid? He'd never

lost anyone except his mother and he'd been a tod-
dler at the time, so he had no memory of the event.

"We were inseparable," he went on. "Sparky was
our constant companion all through childhood. I was
away in college when he went to doggie heaven as
Claire bravely informed me by phone."

Halle hadn't stopped smiling since he'd started
talking. "I didn't realize how lonely being an only
child could be until Andy was gone. We were like
you and Claire. We did everything together." She
laughed. "We even got married once."

Images of a little red-haired girl and blond-haired
boy exchanging childish vows sifted through his
mind. "What brought this on at such an early age?"

"My family and I attended a wedding. I wanted
a dress just like the one the bride wore. The whole
ceremony enthralled me. As soon as I got back home
I informed Andy that we had to have a wedding. He
was always happy to accommodate me. I dug my
mother's wedding dress out of the keepsake trunk in
her room." Halle shook her head. "I think I almost
gave her a heart attack. At least I didn't damage it."

Silence lapsed between them. He might have only
met this woman a few hours ago, but he knew what
she was feeling. He knew what she wanted, and he
couldn't give it to her. It hurt him to think of hurting her.

"I'm not the long-lost kid you're looking for,
Halle. Today is my first trip to Winchester. I can
see how badly you want this story to somehow have

a happy ending but I can't be that happy ending for you. I'm just a guy from California who received a strange piece of mail about a missing kid." A strange piece of mail that had him hopping on a plane.

"Can I tell you something else?"

He heaved a big breath. "Sure, why not?"

"Andy had a dog named Sparky, too. He went missing just a couple of weeks before Andy. There were people who worried that Andy had gone off looking for Sparky and couldn't find his way back home. Of course that wasn't true." She shrugged. She'd been holding this back since the moment he showed her that photo of his dog. "Your Sparky looks exactly like Andy's Sparky. Tell me that isn't a hell of a coincidence."

He held up his hands. "You didn't mention a dog before I did." Had she deliberately withheld that information or conjured it up to keep him interested?

"We hadn't gotten that far. The subject hadn't come up. But there are photos I can show you."

"This is too much." He shook his head.

"There's one way we can potentially rule you out."

His gaze narrowed. "I'm happy to leave a DNA sample, but I can't hang around to wait for results."

"I wasn't thinking about DNA, but I will gladly take a sample to the lab. Thanks for offering."

He'd walked right into that one. "What did you have in mind?"

"Andy had a birthmark."

Liam digested the statement. "If that's the case, then you can rule me out now because I don't have any birthmarks."

This news should have made him feel relieved. Strangely it did not.

"You might not be aware you have one," she countered. "And there's always the possibility that it has faded. You—Andy still had it when he was seven. Usually this particular type of birthmark is gone by the age of one. If it stays, it's usually there for good."

He held his hands up as if in surrender. "So where was this hidden birthmark?" Now he was just irritated. He had really allowed this thing to go too far. He should have left after their meeting in her office.

What the hell was he doing here?

She scooted off her stool and went around to his right side. "It was in the hairline just behind his right ear."

Her hands reached toward him and he froze.

"I'm sorry," she shook her head. "May I look? I'll have to touch you to do that."

He nodded, suddenly unsure of his voice.

Her fingers felt cool against his skin as she swiped the tips through his hair. The new thread of tension roiling through him annoyed him further. Of course he wouldn't be aware of a birthmark in a place like that. If he did have one, maybe she had seen it and was making the whole thing up. This could be her way of launching her story into the stratosphere. He didn't know this woman. She could be—

The sound of her breath catching derailed his next thought. Her fingers fell away from him.

Liam turned to look at her. "What?"

Eyes wide, lips parted, she pressed her fingers to her mouth and stepped back.

Fury, hot and unreasonable, erupted inside him. "Show me," he demanded.

Without a word she walked to the door on the left side of her bed, turned on a light and left the door open for him to follow.

He stepped into the bathroom as if he were crossing into enemy territory. She pulled a mirror from a shelf above the toilet and passed it to him.

The maneuver was awkward and it took a minute, but he finally got his head, arms and the mirror positioned just right so he could see what had freaked her out.

The pinkish mark was shaped like upside down lips.

"It's called an angel's kiss," she said, her voice whisper thin. "This is the exact same shape, color and placement as the one Andy had."

He wasn't doing this. It was ridiculous. A sham, a trick to help her further her career. Why had he been so stupid, coming here?

He carefully placed the mirror on the counter and turned to face her. "I have to go now."

He squeezed past her and stormed across the

room. His hand was on the doorknob, ready to turn, when her voice stopped him.

"Let me get my keys."

Damn it. He closed his eyes, wanted to kick himself. He'd left his rental at her office.

He waited while she gathered her bag and her keys. She led the way down the metal staircase attached to the side of the garage. He stayed behind her, not wanting to engage in conversation. All he wanted was out of here. They reached her car on the next street and they both got in without speaking. His plan to avoid any further discussion worked until she pulled away from the curb and he was a captive audience.

"I don't know how you can continue to pretend there isn't a strong possibility that you're Andy Clark," she said firmly.

"My name is Liam Hart." He stared into the night.

"I can't force you to believe what I'm telling you." She sighed. "But I knew it was you as soon as you walked into my office."

"Stop."

She said no more, and he was grateful she left it at that. They drove in silence across the quiet town. The businesses on the square were closed for the night. Traffic was near nonexistent. When she turned into the parking lot behind the newspaper building, he relaxed just a little.

"Give me your cell number," she said simply.

"Here." She gave him her phone to enter his number.

When he didn't respond, she said, quietly, "Please. In case I get more information."

After a pause, he did as she asked. Then placed the device on the console between them.

"There's a hotel near the Kroger on Dinah Shore Boulevard. There's an inn but it's farther out of the downtown area." She braked to a stop, slid the gearshift into Park.

"I'll find it." He reached for the door handle.

"Whatever you or I believe, Liam," she said, waylaying him, "someone sent that article to you. Someone knows something about you and your past. Maybe something you don't even know, the way you didn't know about the birthmark. You can't just walk away from this."

"Yes, I can. Coming here was a mistake." He opened the door.

"Andy's mother is sick. She needs to know," she said. "Are you going to just walk away and pretend it doesn't matter one way or the other?"

He looked at her then. "Yes."

He climbed out of her car and strode to his. This wild-goose chase was over.

GETTING A ROOM was quick and easy.

He threw his bag onto the bed and collapsed next to it. He closed his eyes and struggled to banish all the voices and images from his head. None of this was real. It couldn't be real. This must be a mistake. Someone's twisted idea of a joke.

His cell vibrated and he tugged it from his pocket. If it was Halle…

Claire.

"Hey."

"Why haven't you called me? I've been going crazy with worry. What did you find out? Did that reporter send you the article?"

He rubbed his head with his free hand. God, he needed a drink. "I was having dinner with the reporter and her family, and no, she didn't send me the article. That part is still a mystery."

The dead air space told him that his mystery-loving sister was not satisfied.

"I should have come with you. I'm better at this sort of thing than you."

"Claire—"

"I've been through all the family papers. All the photo albums. I'm telling you there are no photos of you between when you were a baby and seven years old. Something is wrong with this, Liam. You have a right to know what that is."

"What if I don't want to know?" There was no way he was telling her about the birthmark. Lots of kids had birthmarks. So what if he had the same kind in the same place as this Andy Clark? That didn't mean anything.

"You're in denial. I should call Mom. She has to know what really happened. If this is some ridiculous joke someone is playing on you, she'll know. If it's not, she'll know."

"Do you actually think she would tell you if she and Dad stole a seven-year-old kid? Come on now, Claire. That's a little far-fetched even for you."

"Is it? It wouldn't be the first secret they kept from us."

This was unfortunately true. They'd kept the news about his dad's illness a secret until he was hardly able to get out of the bed.

Liam recalled another incident that Claire wouldn't remember. When Liam was twelve he'd made friends with the son of one of the summer workers. The kid and his father suddenly disappeared—didn't show up for work, rental house was empty—and Liam's father had said they'd had to leave because of a family emergency. Later, Liam had overheard some of the workers whispering about how the boy had been a kidnap victim. The parents had divorced and the father had disappeared with him to prevent the mother from getting sole custody. When Liam demanded the truth from his father, he'd explained that he was concerned Liam would be traumatized by the news.

He'd been traumatized all right. It was the first time his father had lied to him.

Or was it?

"I'll be back tomorrow," Liam said. He didn't want to talk about this anymore.

"See you then but I'm still phoning Mom," his sister warned.

Liam ended the call and fell back on the bed. He

needed rest, oblivion. He had hardly dozed since receiving that article.

A good night's sleep would give him a new perspective.

THEN

"ALL I HAVE to do is say I do?"

This was kind of weird but if it made Halle happy, he was cool with it. She was his best friend.

"Yes. I'll ask a question and you say 'I do.' Then you ask me a question and I say 'I do.'"

Her wild hair was like a lion's mane framing her face. It made him smile. Sometimes when they were watching TV he would try his best to count her freckles. He always lost count. Kind of like when they tried counting stars.

"Okay." He smiled. "Ask me and I'll say it."

Halle straightened her dress. It was really her mother's dress. It was all white and had lots of lace. He'd never seen Mrs. Lane wear it before. No matter that it was way too big, Halle looked pretty.

"Give me a minute to remember," she said, making a face like she was concentrating real hard.

"Oh yeah. Do you take this woman—" she pointed to her chest "—that's me, to be your lif'ful wedded wife?"

He frowned. "What's lif'ful?"

She shook her head, her hair flying with the move. "I dunno. Just say I do."

He nodded. "I do."

She grinned. "Now you ask me."

"Do you take this woman—" he began.

"Not woman, silly," she chided. "Man! You're the man."

"Oh yeah. Do you take this man to be your lif'ful wedded wife?"

She rolled her eyes and groaned. "Husband, not wife!"

He laughed so hard he couldn't breathe.

Her face told him he was not funny.

"Okay, okay. Do you take this man to be your lif'ful wedded husband?"

Her grin was back. "I do!"

He stood there a moment. "Now what?"

"Ah…oh yeah. Now I 'nounce you husband and wife."

"Does that mean we're married now?"

She frowned. "Wait. There's one more part. You gotta kiss the bride."

He glanced around, confused. "What's a bride?"

"Me, silly!"

"Oh." He frowned. "Like on the lips?"

She nodded.

He shrugged. "That's kind of gross, but okay."

She closed her eyes, her lips puckered and lifted toward him.

This was the silliest thing…

He wiped his mouth, puckered his lips and leaned

forward. He kissed her the way his mom always kissed him. Just a quick touch of lips.

She opened her eyes and smiled. "Now we're married forever and ever."

Chapter Five

NOW

Nancy Clark drew the covers back and sat down on the bed. She was tired tonight. More tired than usual.

She looked around the room. She'd pulled all those boxes down from the top shelf of the closet, which was probably why she was so tired. A woman her age had no business climbing up and down from a chair.

But she'd needed to look. To hold those precious keepsakes just once more.

Halle had promised to come back any time she wanted to start part two of her story—Andy's story, really. Nancy had decided to call her tomorrow. She would show her the things in the boxes and she would tell her the rest of the story. All of it, not leaving a single part out.

It was time.

She'd seen him on the back porch of the Lane

home. She'd been sitting in the dark on her own back porch, watching. Her patience had paid off. She'd gotten to see him three times. Going into the Lane home, going out to Halle's apartment over the garage and then again as he'd left for the night.

He was so handsome. He had grown into a fine man. Andrew would be proud.

Goodness, how she missed him. After two years one would expect that she'd gotten used to being alone, but that was not the case. She missed her husband. Wept for him every night. As hard as she tried to maintain her composure, she would lie down at night, and just as she drifted off, the memories would fill her head. He had loved her so much. Been so good to her even after that horrible day.

Andrew had been a fine husband. A very good father.

It had hurt the two of them to go on after that day, but it had been the right thing to do. They had both recognized how important it was to press forward. Looking back would only add to their pain.

She sighed and fluffed her pillow, then turned off the lamp on the bedside table. She always slept with the door open and the bathroom light on. The glow filtering into the hallway cut the darkness without being right in her face. At her age, she didn't want to go stumbling around in the dark.

Tomorrow she would call Halle and maybe she would get to see him up close. Touch him even. Wouldn't that be nice? Then she would have Judith take her to the cemetery so she could tell Andrew all about it.

Their boy was home.

A shadow suddenly blocked the light.

Nancy's head jerked up. She couldn't see the face but someone was standing in her doorway. She yelped and grabbed for the lamp on the bedside table. One tug of the chain and it came on.

Then she recognized him, even after so many years. "What're you doing here?"

"We had a deal, Nancy. You and I and Andrew. Andrew kept his end of the deal, took it to the grave with him, but it appears you have not."

He moved a step closer to the bed and she wished the telephone extension was on her side of the bed, but it was not. It was on Andrew's side. She had never moved it.

"I...I don't know what you're talking about."

"Yes, you do. The one rule was that you were never to speak of it again. Never. To no one. Not even each other."

But they had. She and Andrew had spoken about it many times, inside with the doors and windows closed and the lights turned out.

"I haven't told anyone. You read the article. You know what I told the reporter. Nothing important."

He glanced around her room, spotted the baby blanket. "Oh, Nancy. Dear Nancy. You brought him back here and now there will be questions. A new investigation, perhaps. This won't do. It won't do at all."

Courage rose inside her. "We made a mistake. All of us. What you did to that…that woman was on you. We didn't ask you to do that."

He moved closer still.

Nancy pulled the bedcovers to her chest as if the well-washed cotton could somehow protect her.

"But I did and now we have a problem."

Fear crept up her spine. "It's your problem, not mine."

He nodded. "You're correct and now I'm going to fix it."

Chapter Six

Friday, March 13

Halle grabbed her shoulder bag, tucked her phone inside and started for the door. She'd hardly slept last night. She'd wanted to call him or go to the hotel and shake him, make him listen.

He was being unreasonable. This was all strange and unsettling but there was no point in denying what was obvious. Liam Hart was Andy Clark.

Her cell rang and she tugged it from her bag as she reached the door. *Mom* flashed on the screen. Frowning, she accepted the call. "Hey, Mom, what's up?"

"I know you're probably getting ready to leave for work."

"Leaving now," Halle confirmed. Her mother's voice sounded strange. "Is everything okay?"

"The police and an ambulance are next door. Your father has gone over to find out what's happened."

Was Mrs. Clark ill? Why hadn't she called for help? Halle and her parents had urged her over the years to call if she ever needed anything. "I'm heading there now."

Halle ended the call and shoved the phone back into her bag. She hurried out the door, almost forgot to lock it and double-timed it down the stairs. Poor Mrs. Clark, all alone and unable to protect or help herself. As she reached the front yard, another vehicle was turning into the drive next door.

The bold lettering on the side of the van stopped her cold.

CORONER.

"Oh, God." Ice gushed through her veins.

Her feet were suddenly moving again. She bounded across Mrs. Clark's yard, up the steps and onto the porch. Halle was through the open front door before the officer who was supposed to be guarding the scene noticed her. He was at the far end of the porch, vomiting.

The coppery odor of blood filled her lungs the instant she hit the hallway beyond the living room.

Low voices echoed from the kitchen. Halle changed directions and went into the kitchen instead of down the hall to the bedrooms. Eileen Brewster sat at the table, her face in her hands. Eileen cleaned house for Mrs. Clark once a week. Always on Fridays. A lump swelled in Halle's throat.

The man talking to Eileen looked up. Chief of Police William Brannigan—Billy, everyone called him.

"What's going on, Chief?" Her voice sounded oddly small. She suddenly wondered where her father was.

"Halle," he said with a nod. "Your daddy is out on the back porch. Maybe you should go out there and talk to him for a minute while Ms. Brewster and I finish up."

Halle nodded and moved quickly through the room. Brannigan's voice softened once more as he spoke gently to Eileen.

Howard Lane stood at the railing, looking out over the Clarks' backyard as well as their own. She and Andy used to stand on their porches at night and send each other flashlight signals. When Halle neared her father she saw the dampness on his cheeks. Oh no. Oh no.

"What happened, Daddy?"

He looked up, pulled Halle into his arms. "Someone came into the house last night and killed Nancy."

Halle drew back. "Oh my God. Who would do such a thing? Was it a robbery?"

Her father shook his head. "We don't know yet. The house wasn't ransacked. But boxes had been taken out of her closet and sat around the floor in her bedroom."

"Eileen found her?" Poor Eileen. Halle could only imagine the horror.

Howard nodded. "After several knocks on the door with no answer, she figured Nancy was away from the house for some reason, so she unlocked the door and let herself in. She said whoever killed her had taken a knife and cut her throat right there in her own bed."

Halle blinked fast, imagining the horror of it. She couldn't conceive anyone hurting Mrs. Clark. She had never done anything to hurt anyone. She was a beloved fixture in their community. The poor woman who lost her only child.

"This is crazy." Her next thought was that now Nancy would never know that Andy was still alive. No matter whether Liam wanted to believe or not, Halle was certain. He was the lost boy.

The back door opened and Chief Brannigan came outside. "Howard, can you take Eileen home? She's in no condition to drive."

"Sure. Sure." Howard scrubbed at his face. "Your mother's going to be devastated."

Halle agreed. Though Nancy and Judith hadn't been as close since Andy vanished, they were still good friends.

When her father was gone, Chief Brannigan turned to Halle. "I read your article."

Halle managed a nod. "Audrey told me." Her boss had said that the chief and the sheriff had read the article with interest.

"I told Audrey I was happy to let Luther Holcomb know you wanted to talk to him whenever you're ready."

"I would appreciate that, Chief. Mrs. Clark was excited about the possibility of finally finding the rest of the story."

"She had pulled out a bunch of boxes from her closet. Did she do that for you?"

Halle shook her head. "We talked, looked at photo albums but nothing more. When I came by on Sunday, she wanted to show me something in Andy's room. A photo of the two of us that had been his favorite. I passed her room on the way to Andy's and there were no boxes then. Just the bed and a dresser, a couple of nightstands."

The officer who'd been vomiting came around the corner of the house. "Burt's taking the body now, Chief."

"Good. Thanks, Sails." Brannigan turned to Halle. "I need to speak with Burt for a moment and then I'll be right back. Before I go, can you tell me if this visitor from California—this Liam Hart—is still in Winchester?"

"I'm not sure. He has a flight back home leaving from Nashville today, but he didn't say what time. He may still be at the hotel."

"If he's still here, see if you can get him to my office."

Halle stared after the chief as he strode back inside. Why would the chief of police want to talk to

Liam? Who'd mentioned him to Brannigan—her father?

Certainly he had nothing to do with Mrs. Clark's death...

Halle drew out her phone and made the call. It went to voice mail. She hung up and called again. He could be at breakfast or in the shower. This time she left a message. "Liam, this is Halle. Something's happened." She decided not to tell him about the murder. "Chief of Police Brannigan would like to meet with you in his office at City Hall. If you haven't left yet, please come. I'll be there, too." She hesitated. Instead of goodbye, she said, "See you there."

By the time Halle put her phone away, the chief was back at the door. "You mind coming inside again?"

Rather than answer, she followed him inside. He paused in the middle of the kitchen, his trademark hat on the table.

"Audrey told me this Liam fellow showed up with a copy of your article that someone apparently sent him anonymously."

At least that explained how he knew about Liam's arrival.

Before she could say anything, he said, "Ro and I had dinner with Audrey and Colt last night. She wanted to bring me up to speed."

Tanya, Halle decided. She hadn't spoken to Audrey about Liam until this morning. Tanya must have told her after he barged into the office last evening. Since Audrey hadn't known the rest until this morning, Brannigan had obviously called her after coming here.

"Did you speak to her again this morning?" Halle asked to confirm her conclusion.

"I did. After I saw what had been done to Mrs. Clark, I called Audrey to find out if she knew anything more about his visit."

This was wrong, wrong, wrong. "Chief, you're not thinking that he had anything to do with this?"

He held her gaze for a moment before saying, "I'm only thinking that he might have felt compelled to visit her. Which could explain all those boxes pulled down from the top shelf in her closet. If he visited her and she was still alive, I need to know if she mentioned anyone else who planned to come by or if he saw a vehicle parked on the street."

Reasonable, Halle decided. "I got his voice mail when I called just now. If he hasn't left yet, I'm assuming he'll show up at your office."

"When you were in Nashville, I'm sure you were at homicide scenes from time to time."

She nodded. "Lots of times."

"I'd like you to see something."

Adrenaline lit in her veins, whether fueled by anticipation or dread, she couldn't say. "All right."

As they moved through the house, she saw the crime scene technician. He and Eileen must have parked on the street because she hadn't noticed their cars in the driveway. Then again, she had been focused on getting into the house. Perhaps she simply hadn't been looking.

The odor of blood was stronger as they neared Mrs. Clark's bedroom. Andy's room was at the end of the hall. The family bathroom was on the left, along with another bedroom that Nancy had used for a sewing room.

The bed linens were covered in blood. More blood was spattered on the carpet. Halle kept the idea that this was Mrs. Clark's blood pushed aside. She focused on the details of the room. Gold drapes pulled tightly closed. Bedside table on each side of the bed. Lamps with beige shades adorned with gold fringe sat on the tables. A dresser stood on the wall next to the closet door. Beyond the bed on the far side of the room near the windows were boxes stacked on the floor. Three medium-sized boxes, the kind used for moving. The tape had been cut and the lids pulled open.

"Try not to step in the blood."

Halle followed him, careful of the crimson stains on the beige carpet.

The first thing she noticed about the boxes was a baby blanket lying on the top of whatever was inside one. The blanket was blue with a monogramed A in a lighter blue. Andy's baby blanket.

Brannigan pulled a pair of latex gloves from his jacket pocket and handed them to her. "Have a look at that box, the one closest to the bed, if you would."

Halle tugged on the gloves and moved closer to the boxes. The first box, the one with the baby blanket, appeared to be filled with stuffed animals and other toys. The next one had neatly folded clothes. Boy clothes. Andy's clothes. The ones he wore before he vanished.

The third box held another, smaller box. Halle reached inside the smaller box. Photographs. She shuffled through the loose photos. Most were of Andy. Others included Nancy and Andrew. And sure enough, there were photos with Sparky, too. She lifted the smaller box from the larger one and set it atop one of the others. Beneath that smaller box was yet another box; this one was really small and nestled amid more clothes.

She reached for the much smaller box and opened it. It was more like a gift box made for a scarf or perfume set. Inside were more photos.

Her heart stumbled.

There were photos of Andy. But not seven-year-old or younger Andy. These were Andy when he was older. Like ten and twelve. Fifteen…twenty. Halle's mouth went bone-dry. The fully grown Andy… *Liam*.

No question. He wore another tee that sported the logo of the Hart family winery.

How was this possible? "Why would she have these?"

Brannigan's voice dragged her attention from the disturbing contents of the box.

"I don't know." A realization suddenly expanded

through her mind, stealing her breath. Could Mrs. Clark have been the one to mail him the article?

If she knew where Andy was, why didn't she do something? Why didn't she tell Halle during the interview?

"We need to speak to Liam Hart," Brannigan said.

Halle shook her head. "But he insists he's never been here before."

Not possible. She understood this without a single doubt. He was Andy. He had to be. There simply was no other alternative. He either truly didn't know or he was hiding the truth for some reason. Perhaps protecting someone he had grown to love in his new life.

"He may not have been here," Brannigan offered, "but Mrs. Clark has either been to see him or had someone watching him."

This made no sense whatsoever.

She stared at the blood on the bed. What in the world had Mrs. Clark not told her?

LIAM PICKED UP his bag, took one last look around the room and headed for the door. He'd made it across the parking lot and into his rental car before curiosity got the better of him and he listened to Halle's voice mail.

He'd been in the shower when she called. He'd told himself it didn't matter what she had to say, but somehow it did. He wasn't sure how just yet, but there was this feeling—this annoying little voice—that wouldn't turn loose. It nagged at him like an errant weed choking at one of his grape vines, a weed that just wouldn't be thwarted.

He set the phone to speaker and hit Play. Her voice sounded strained, uncertain, worried. Nothing like the confident reporter he'd met.

The chief of police wanted to meet with him.

What? Why would Liam meet with anyone here, much less the chief of police? Did the people in this town want to solve this cold case so badly that they were grasping at straws? Surely that urgency didn't extend to the chief of police.

The little nagging voice that would not be silenced nudged him.

He blew out a big breath. The last thing he wanted was for trouble from Winchester to follow him back to California. Claire would be upset and Penelope would be hurt that he'd even come here like this. He had plenty of time before his 3 p.m. flight. He might as well get this meeting or whatever the hell it was over with.

Last night he'd managed to get himself lost finding his way to the boulevard. Seemed ridiculous in a town this small but it had happened, even with GPS. In view of Halle's call this morning, that turned out to be a good thing. He had passed City Hall while driving around and around the town square until he made the proper turn. Winchester's town square was somewhat like a big city roundabout but not as easily maneuvered—at least not for a stranger.

He turned left out of the parking lot, heading for downtown Winchester. He'd barely slept at all. He'd dreamed of a little girl with crazy red curls in a wedding dress. Her smile and those sparkling green eyes had mesmerized him. Or had it been Andy Clark in the dream? The kid looked so damned much like him it was difficult to say one way or another.

He shook off the frustrating notion. Being in this place, spending time with the reporter, it had all somehow managed to put strange ideas in his head. Why was that? Why was he susceptible to these bizarre feelings? He couldn't remember a time in his life that he ever doubted who he was or from where he'd come.

Why now? Was this some sort of early midlife crisis?

A delayed reflex to his father's death?

Or maybe he was just losing it. Stress could do that, right? Shelly had a valid point. He'd been working seven days a week for months. Maybe he did need a real vacation.

As soon as he got back home, he and Claire were going to have a long talk about the future and putting themselves first from time to time.

He parked at City Hall and climbed out of the rental. Two slots away he spotted Halle's car. She was here already. Good. At least he would know someone in the room.

Wait, did he really know her?

For all he knew, this could be all her fault. The ruthless journalist who wanted to get the story regardless of the price to others. But that wasn't her way. He'd read a good deal about her. Yeah, it was stuff on the internet, but he hadn't read anything to suggest she was that sort of heartless reporter. She certainly could have saved her career had she chosen to lie and throw her sources under the bus during those last two big assignments. Instead, she had refused and her career had crashed and burned. If anything, someone else had set out to screw her over.

But she'd let it go. Came home and started over.

Maybe she was a nice person.

He entered the lobby and came immediately face-to-face with a security checkpoint. A cold, hard reality of today's world.

"Keys, phone and anything else in your pockets goes in the tray," the uniformed officer told him as he approached. "Belt, too, if you're wearing one."

"No belt," Liam assured him. Keys, phone, a couple of quarters went into the tray.

"Very good, sir. Just step through the metal detector and you're all done."

Liam walked through without setting off any buzzers. He collected his stuff and asked, "Where can I find the chief's office?"

The officer gave him directions and Liam started that way. The City Hall was a piece of vintage architecture from the early part of the last century.

The soft soles of his sneakers were soundless on the marble floor. He pushed through the double doors sporting the Winchester Police Department logo and walked to the receptionist's desk.

"Mr. Hart?"

Apparently they were waiting for him. "Yes."

"This way, sir."

She escorted him to a conference room. Two men and Halle sat around the table. All, including Halle, stood as he entered the room. The receptionist turned to him and asked if he needed anything to drink. Water? Coffee?

"No, thanks." His full attention was on the three already in the room.

"Liam," Halle said, "this is Chief of Police William Brannigan." She gestured to the man on her left, then to the one on her right. "And this is Detective Clarence Lincoln. Gentlemen, this is Liam Hart of Napa, California."

Both men shook his hand. Brannigan gestured to an empty chair. "Have a seat, Mr. Hart, and we'll go over the reason I asked you to stop by."

It was nine already. As long as he was out of here by noon he had no problem listening to whatever the two men had to say.

When they'd all settled, Brannigan placed a photo on the table. The woman pictured was older, maybe seventy or so.

"Have you ever met this woman?"

Liam shook his head. "I haven't, no."

From the same folder he'd pulled the first photo, he pulled a second, placed it on top of the first. "What about this woman?"

His gaze rested on the woman's face. She looked to be forty or so. Blond hair, gray eyes. His gut tightened. She looked vaguely familiar. But he couldn't say he'd ever met her before.

"Sorry." He turned his hands up. "I don't know her, either."

Halle looked from Liam to Brannigan.

"What's this about?" He suddenly felt edgy, his nerves raw. His patience thinning.

"This woman—" Brannigan tapped the second photo "—is the same as the first. Nancy Clark, Andy Clark's mother."

Liam blinked, unsure of what to say or do at first. Then he shook his head. "I don't mean to be rude, but why are you showing these photos to me? Whatever Miss Lane has suggested, I am not Andy Clark."

Brannigan nodded once. "That may be so," he said. "But you arrived in Winchester yesterday afternoon. Spent some time with Miss Lane and her family. Then you went to the hotel. Is that right?"

What the hell? "Of course it's right." He looked to Halle. "She drove me to my car at the newspaper. I drove from there to the hotel. I stayed all night. Left the hotel and drove here." He avoided looking at Halle, focused on Brannigan instead. He asked again, "What is this about?"

"Nancy Clark lived next door to Halle and her family."

The fact that he used the past tense put Liam on alert.

"Around midnight last night she was murdered."

Liam couldn't speak. He thought of several things to say. *I hate to hear this but I didn't know her. My condolences to the family.* None of those words would rise from his tongue. His throat seemed to be closing and his stomach churned. He remembered Halle's words from last night, about Mrs. Clark being ill, and didn't he want to see her.

"Whoever broke into her house was knowledgeable in breaking and entering without leaving any evidence behind. The perpetrator walked into her bedroom and cut her throat, leaving her alone to bleed out and die."

Sweat formed on Liam's skin. "Robbery?" he managed to ask, his voice sounding unnatural. His mouth and throat were dry.

Brannigan shook his head. "Nothing was taken."

"We believe," the detective on the other side of the table spoke for the first time, "her murder was related to the article that brought you here."

Liam scrubbed a hand over his mouth. He felt sick. Really sick. "Where is your—" he stood, his chair rolling back, bumping into another "—bathroom?"

"To the left," Brannigan said. "Fourth door on the right."

Liam rushed out of the room. His body shook so hard it was difficult to walk straight. He shoved through the door marked Men and went to the sink. He braced his hands on the cold porcelain and stared at his reflection. His gut roiled mercilessly. Turning on the faucet, he splashed cold water on his face.

Didn't help.

Bile burned in his throat.

He hurried to the nearest stall and vomited the hot sourness from his gut.

Hands braced on his knees, he took a minute to stop gagging, no matter that there was nothing in his stomach beyond the coffee and bitterness that had already spewed out of him.

"What the hell?" he muttered.

He flushed the toilet and went back to the sink to wash his face again. He cupped a hand and caught water to rinse his mouth, then used a paper towel to wipe the newly formed sweat from his face.

"Pull it together, man," he said to his reflection. None of this had anything to do with him. He was just overtired, stressed, and he'd let all that speculation Halle tossed at him get under his skin.

Deep breath and he was ready to get this done so he could get out of here.

Back in the conference room, the three waited. If they'd talked about him while he was gone, they didn't let on now.

"How about a bottle of water?" Lincoln asked. Rather than wait for an answer, he reached across the table and sat one in front of Liam as if he comprehended exactly what had transpired in the men's room.

Liam didn't trust himself to drink a drop for fear it would spew out of him again.

"Just so we're clear," Brannigan said. "We're not accusing you of anything, Mr. Hart. We've already spoken to management at your hotel. You checked in at ten and didn't leave your room until, as you stated, you came here this morning."

This was ludicrous. "Are you saying I was a suspect?"

"Yes," Lincoln answered for him. "The article goes viral. Stranger comes to town. The missing child's mother—his only living parent—is murdered. We wouldn't be very good at our jobs if we hadn't suspected you."

Liam nodded. Made some sort of bizarre sense, he supposed. "Is there something else you wanted to talk about? If not, I'd like to be on my way."

"You're free to leave whenever you wish, Mr. Hart." Brannigan shrugged. "I have no legal grounds to hold you here."

Liam readied to stand. He wanted out of here. The sooner the better.

"But," Brannigan continued, halting his rise from the table, "we believe you're the key. It would mean a great deal to me personally if you would stay a few days and help us figure out what happened."

Liam shook his head. "How can I possibly help you?"

His heart was pounding again, sweat beading to the point of sliding down his skin. Maybe he had food poisoning. No offense to Halle's mom but something was wrong with him and he hadn't eaten since having dinner with the Lanes.

"I honestly don't know," Brannigan admitted. "Maybe you can't. But Detective Lincoln and I believe someone thinks you can. The story on Andy appeared in the paper. You're sent a copy of it from an anonymous source. You come to town. Mrs. Clark is murdered. We think there's a connection between all this."

How the hell could he just walk away from that?

He couldn't.

Chapter Seven

NOW

Halle didn't really have an appetite. Lunch was more or less a way to pass the time until the evidence tech was finished at Mrs. Clark's house. Chief Brannigan had given her permission to look through the house, as well as the boxes in the bedroom, for any useful information. Halle's mother, Judith, was the executor of Mrs. Clark's will and since the poor lady had no other family, it would be up to Halle's family to pack up her home.

Unless they proved that Liam was Andy. Then the property would go to him. Substantiating his true identity would change everything. If only Mrs. Clark had lived to meet him.

Halle's gaze landed on the man across the table from her in the small café near the center of town. She'd suggested he join her after the tense meeting with the police chief. Still dazed, he'd agreed, but she suspected only because he simply didn't know what else to do.

He was still in denial. No matter that the woman's death—a woman he insisted he had never met—had shaken him to the core. He'd gone pale when the chief told him the news. He'd rushed to the men's room. Somewhere deep inside him, memories obviously had stirred. Possibly he hadn't understood his reaction or perhaps refused to accept it for what it was, but it meant something far more than he wanted to see just now.

The tiny fragments of evidence were slowly coming together.

"Thanks for agreeing to have lunch with me," she said when he continued to stare at the menu. It wasn't that extensive or that interesting. His continued perusal was about avoiding eye contact and conversation.

Understandable, in view of the fact that he'd been considered and then ruled out as a homicide suspect. The news was enough to unsettle even the strongest guy. Watching this sort of thing on television or in a movie was vastly different from experiencing it in real life.

"I'm sorry you had to go through that in the chief's office."

He looked at her then. "I've only had one speeding ticket in my life. Nothing else. I've damned sure never been suspected of murder." His head moved side to side as his gaze dropped back to the menu.

She sighed, set her menu aside. She ate here all the time; it wasn't like she didn't know what she preferred to order—even if she wasn't hungry.

"The burritos are the best in town," she said, deciding to press on. "I rarely eat tacos but the ones here are really good."

He placed his menu atop hers. "Sounds like the best way to go."

Spotting their shift away from the menus, the waitress appeared. "Ready to order?"

Liam waited for Halle to go first. She imagined he wasn't hungry, either. But eating would pass the time, would occupy their hands and mouths. "Veggie burrito," Halle announced. "No extra sauce, please. Water to drink."

He requested the same except he wanted the extra sauce. The waitress picked up their menus and hurried away to turn in their order.

"It wasn't personal," she offered, though she felt confident her reasoning was skewed. "Like Detective Lincoln said, it was just a routine ruling out of possibilities. Standard procedure. Ms. Brewster had a key to her house. My mother does, as well. I'm sure they both had to be ruled out, too."

Okay, he seriously doubted the cleaning lady or Halle's mother were ever considered suspects, but he accepted her attempt to make him feel better.

He made a scoffing sound. "Don't even go there. We both know this was different."

Fair enough. "I suppose you're right."

The waitress arrived with glasses of ice water. Liam thanked her.

As soon as she was gone, he said, "What was that? I don't think I heard you."

Halle rolled her eyes. "You're right."

He executed a nod of acknowledgement. "I feel better now."

She couldn't help herself; she laughed.

"What now, besides lunch, I mean?" he inquired.

"I'm hoping that by the time we're done with lunch, we can go inside the Clark home and have a look at personal papers and photos." She hadn't told him about the photos she'd found of him after he was abducted. This was something he needed to see with his own eyes. She sensed he needed to absorb these truths slowly, through his own observations.

Or maybe she just didn't want to be the one to tell him.

Coward.

"I heard you discussing the possibility with the police chief, but I wasn't sure his agreement included me."

"I assumed it did," she fudged. If he was Andy Clark, he should have access to what was rightfully his. "If you don't mind, we'll go with my assessment."

"You're the boss." He shrugged. "For now."

Halle laughed. "You always let me be the boss."

The words were hardly out of her mouth when

she realized her mistake. "I'm sorry. It was just a random voiced thought."

He held her gaze but he didn't bother to argue or to refute her words.

"Andy always went with whatever I wanted to do," she explained, then she smiled. "Not because I was always right or had the best ideas. I think he just wanted to indulge me. Even as a child he was a consummate gentleman. Mom used to laugh and say a good husband always did what his wife asked him to do." Halle made a face. "She never let me forget I sneaked her wedding dress out of that trunk."

A smile cracked Liam's serious expression. "I guess you recognized what you wanted even then."

"We were kids. I had a vivid imagination with little or no impulse control. What can I say?"

To Halle's relief the food arrived and keeping the conversation going was no longer necessary.

REPORTERS WERE HELD back at the end of the block. For now, no one except residents was allowed on the stretch of South High where Halle lived and Mrs. Clark had died. She wasn't sure how long this would go on, but Chief Brannigan had said she could go into the house and look around now. Looking was the extent of her access. She wasn't to remove anything from the house. Detective Lincoln would be on hand to bag anything found that appeared connected in any way to Mrs. Clark's murder.

The chief had passed along that Mrs. Clark's body

would be ready for pickup from the coroner's office sometime next week. Halle's mother had already called DuPont Funeral Home to take care of the final arrangements. DuPont's had taken care of Mr. Clark. Of course his wife would want the same. As it turned out, Mrs. Clark already had prearrangements with DuPont's. Judith was grateful not to have to make all the selections.

Halle had given Liam one of her father's ball caps that she kept in her car to wear, in an effort to avoid the prying eyes and cameras of the reporters. She parked in Mrs. Clark's drive. Halle's mother was already there with Detective Lincoln.

When Halle shut off her car she turned to Liam. "You ready?"

"Sure." He reached for the door.

"Just remember," Halle offered, "sometimes we don't understand what makes the people we care about do the things they do."

He held her gaze, his filled with a resignation that made her regret what he would see inside. But there was no undoing what had been done. She only wished Mrs. Clark were still here to explain.

"If you're trying to tell me something, it's not really coming through."

When she didn't explain further, he got out of the car. She did the same. He waited for her at the porch, always the gentleman.

By the time she reached the porch the door opened and her mother stood there, her face pale, her eyes bright with emotion. Halle went to her and hugged her. The Clarks had lived next door for as long as she could remember. It was like losing a part of the family. It was difficult enough when Mr. Clark passed, but now there was no one left. That era of their lives was over.

Except, she decided as she pulled away from her mother, for the man behind her. And he didn't want to be here. This was not his life. At least not one that he remembered.

For the first time in twenty-five years, Halle fully comprehended that Andy was lost forever. All this time she had told herself that he was somewhere living a good life. All grown up and probably married.

But she had been wrong. Even if she could prove that Liam was Andy, Andy was still gone. The boy she had known, the best friend she'd had, was gone forever. A new sadness settled inside her.

"Let's get started," Judith offered. She smiled at Liam. "It's nice to see you again, despite the circumstances."

He managed a smile and a single nod.

Inside, Detective Lincoln waited. He passed around gloves. "We've already finished the evidence gathering but it's best if we wear gloves anyway."

Latex snapped into place on hands, the sound somber in the quiet house.

"Ms. Brewster confirmed that nothing was missing," Lincoln explained. "She's been cleaning house for Mrs. Clark for twenty years. If anything was taken, it was something hidden that she had never seen before."

Judith nodded. "I walked through the house and I didn't see anything so much as out of place."

"Except those boxes," Halle pointed out.

"Right," Judith agreed. "Even those were permanent fixtures in Nancy's closet. I helped her get one down once when she wanted a box of photos from hers and Andrew's early life. That one is still in the closet."

They progressed to the hall, like a funeral party moving toward the cemetery. Halle paused at Mrs. Clark's bedroom door. "Maybe we should start in Andy's room. Have a look around before we dig into those boxes."

Judith looked surprised at the idea.

Lincoln nodded. "Wherever you believe is the best place to start."

Halle walked to the end of the hall. She wanted Liam in this room before he had a look at those pictures. She doubted he would actually be in a reasonable emotional state once he saw those photographs.

Andy's room was just as it had been the day he went missing. Superhero posters on the wall. Framed photographs of him and his family, him and Halle, stood on the dresser, another on his desk. That photo included Sparky. The reading book he'd forgotten to take to school that day was on his desk. Halle had been so jealous of Andy's desk. She had wanted one just like his. She smiled. She'd always wanted to be just like Andy. She'd loved him dearly—as dearly as any seven-year-old could.

Liam touched the school banner thumbtacked to the wall. He wandered around the room, almost restless. Halle found herself watching him rather than inventorying the items in the room. He walked to the closet. Had a look inside at the toys piled into the corner. The sneakers on the floor. The clothes hanging on the old-fashioned rod that extended across the long, narrow space. Old houses weren't known for large closets. He closed the door and moved to the dresser. Opened one drawer, then the next, studied the contents of each without touching anything or commenting.

He stopped at the desk last. This time his fingers slid across the cover of the book, along the blotter pad covered in doodles. He picked up the one framed photo standing there. A picture of Halle and Andy the Christmas before he disappeared. They were grinning, crocheted caps on their heads, Sparky photobombing. They had been so happy. They'd both gotten bicycles for Christmas. All sorts of adventures had been planned for spring and summer.

Liam abruptly turned around as if he'd realized everyone was staring at him, and it was true. Judith looked away. His gaze met Halle's and she didn't hold back the "I told you so" from her eyes.

"Everything in here appears to be in order," Halle announced.

Her movements a little unsteady, Judith turned

and led the way back into the hall. The dozen steps required to reach Mrs. Clark's room had Halle's tension twisting tighter and tighter. She wasn't sure how to prepare for this. Part of her wanted to warn Liam, but the other part—the reporter's instincts—wanted to see his initial, unbiased reaction.

The bloody bed linens were gone. Likely taken as evidence. The mattress was covered with a clean spread and the blood on the floor had vanished, likely Ms. Brewster's doing. She walked to the first box, the one with all the stuffed animals. "We should probably go through each box. Just to make sure there's nothing hidden under things like all these stuffed animals."

She dropped to her knees next to the box. Judith did the same.

Liam joined them, his expression showing how grudgingly he did so. "Why don't we just cut them all open to make sure nothing's hidden inside?"

Halle stared at him. "Is that what you want to do?"

"Are you still playing shrink?" he demanded, his tone bordering on angry. "That's why you insisted on going through the kid's room first, right? You hoped to evoke some life-altering or revealing reaction?"

Judith looked from Liam to Halle. "Why don't we get started?"

"Good idea," Halle mumbled. She didn't want to argue with him. The way he said the words made her feel mean and selfish. She didn't want to be either of those things. She wanted to do this the right way.

One by one they removed the stuffed animals and toys until they reached the bottom of the box. There were no hidden messages or unexpected items. Just Andy's toys.

Liam hardly looked at any of the items he touched. Rather, he just moved them from the box to the floor.

"I guess we can put them back," Halle suggested.

"You think?"

Her gaze connected with his, noted the anger simmering there. She had evoked a reaction from him, all right. Hard as she imagined he tried, his raw emotions wouldn't be contained. She suspected he realized as much, which was why he was angry and immediately looked away after snapping the remark.

Rather than respond, she and her mother began putting the toys and stuffed animals back. Liam hung his head and joined the effort.

The next box was mostly clothes. Again, the process was tedious. Remove, unfold, refold. Then the clothes all went back in. Again they found nothing of interest or that shouldn't be exactly where it was.

Next was the box with the smaller boxes of photos. They moved slowly through those. Liam paid closer attention now. He studied the boy in the photos. Seemed to analyze the parents shown in each.

"I remember this day," Judith said as she picked

up the next photo. "We'd gone to the beach down in Mobile. What a good time we had."

Halle smiled as she moved through the other photos from that trip. "Andy and I buried each other in the sand."

Their attention lingered on the photos for a moment before they placed them back in the box. With that box finished, Halle reached for the one that would change everything. She removed the lid and picked up a photo. Liam did the same. Judith only stared at the ones readily visible on top of the small pile of photos.

"What the hell?" Liam muttered.

Halle looked from a photo to him. "This is you."

He didn't respond. She was right.

"Did she have someone watching me?" He shook his head. "This gets crazier by the minute."

Halle turned to Detective Lincoln. "It appears Mrs. Clark did know Liam. I'm guessing she had someone watching him, sending her pictures."

"If that's correct, then it's possible Mrs. Clark is the one who sent him the article," Lincoln suggested.

Halle looked to her mom. "I agree. Nancy never said anything to you about thinking the person in these photos was Andy?"

"She never showed them to me. You know after that first year, she refused to talk about him." Judith shook her head. "This is astounding. I had no idea." She gestured to the photos. "Someone had to be taking these photos for her. Nancy rarely left home once she gave up on finding Andy. You remember," she said to Halle, "we'd bring their Christmas gifts to them. Birthday cakes. It was as if this house became their tomb long before either one actually died."

Her mother was right. "This is something a private investigator would do," Halle said to the detective.

"It is," he agreed. "Do you know who she used?"

Halle looked to her mother. Judith shrugged. "I know they went to see more than one but I never knew their names."

"Maybe it's time to talk to Mr. Holcomb," Halle said. "He agreed to see me."

"I'll call the chief," Lincoln said.

"LUTHER HOLCOMB IS one of those folks who like living off the grid," Halle explained as she navigated her father's truck along the narrow road that snaked through the backwoods.

Liam was fairly certain this—he surveyed the thick woods around them—was about as off the grid as you could get and still be in the county.

"The chief says he lives off the land and almost never comes into town."

"Let's just hope he doesn't have an issue with strangers," Liam said, working overtime at being amenable. He was still rattled by those photographs.

"The chief called him. He's expecting us."

This news did nothing to make Liam feel more

comfortable. In fact, he was fairly certain he'd never been more uncomfortable.

How the hell had Nancy Clark gotten those pictures of him? Most were taken at his home in California or somewhere on the vineyard. There was one from his high school graduation and then another from his college graduation. His father and sister had been right there with him in those photos. Penelope hadn't been in any but that was probably because she'd always been the one doing the taking.

He'd struggled to maintain his composure as they sifted through photo after photo. His emotions had almost gotten the better of him. Being rude or snippy had never been his way and yet he'd been both today in that poor dead woman's house.

But this was his life they were tinkering with. Causing him to question all that he thought he knew. As much as he had missed his father since his death, he had never wished he were here more than today. He needed him to explain how this was possible. Needed him to make some sort of logic or sense out of all this confusing information.

There was no logic and certainly, no sense to be found.

He was Liam Hart. He was not Andy Clark. Those flashes of familiarity he'd felt in the boy's room and in that house were nothing more than the power of suggestion.

Halle had him doubting himself. She, her mother and even the chief of police had planted these ridiculous seeds of uncertainty. He needed to go home and hug Claire and Penelope. To anchor himself.

He glanced at the woman behind the wheel. But all he'd wanted to do while they were in that house was hug *her*. Hold on to her while he rode out this hurricane of emotions.

But he was terrified that she would pull him under. She wanted him to be Andy. There were moments when weakness got the better of him and he wanted to be Andy for her…for the woman who'd collected pictures of him throughout his life…the one who'd possibly sent him that newspaper clipping, maybe in hopes he would come home to her. But he wasn't that person.

"Here we go." Halle shoved the gearshift into Park and shut off the ignition.

Liam stared at the rustic cabin as they climbed out. An older model pickup sat next to it. The door opened and a man walked out onto the porch. His hair was mostly gray, but it was long, pulled back into a ponytail. He carried a shotgun braced on one shoulder.

"Miss Lane," the former chief of police said, "I haven't seen you since you were a little girl."

"Chief Holcomb." She walked straight up to him and gave him a hug. "You look as if you're in your element."

"I am that," he agreed. "Got the peace and quiet I was looking for. No more cops and robbers for me."

Halle smiled. "Chief, this is Liam Hart. He's here helping me with my investigation into Andy's case."

Luther eyed Liam for a long moment. "When I first saw him climb out of your daddy's truck I thought you'd found Andy." He cocked his head and studied Liam openly. "You look just like him, Mr. Hart."

"That's what they tell me," Liam said. He figured that was a fair and reasonably safe statement.

"I have a couple of questions for you, Chief, if you have a few minutes."

He nodded. "'Course. Come on in." He turned and started back to the door. "It ain't much but it's mine and can't nobody tell me what to do or expect anything from me."

There was something to be said for that, Liam supposed.

Inside, he and Halle sat on a well-worn sofa while Luther settled into a recliner that looked about as old as he was.

"I'd offer you some of my latest batch of shine but I got a feeling y'all ain't the type."

"Thank you," Halle said, "but I'll pass."

Liam held up a hand. "I'm with the lady."

Luther propped his shotgun against the wall next to his chair. "Fire away, Miss Lane."

"You should call me Halle, Chief."

"Well, then you need to call me Luther. I haven't been the chief in a long time."

"Luther," she acknowledged. "I read the case file

from when Andy vanished. I'm convinced by what I read that you did all that was possible to find him. My father still sings your praises."

"Outside the boy's momma and daddy," Luther said, "there is no one who wanted to find him more than I did. But it didn't happen. This was no random abduction. Whoever took him had been watching for a long time, waiting for just the right opportunity. That's why we couldn't find him. The kidnapper had paid attention to every detail. Nothing was left to chance."

Liam thought of the detailed work his father did. When he'd died, Liam had been certain he would never be able to keep the books and operate the winery as meticulously as his father. He certainly would never be as organized as him.

But that didn't mean anything. His father had been a good man—a great man. He would never have stolen a child under any circumstances. No way. The idea was utterly ludicrous.

For a few minutes, they talked about what was already known, the time and place of the abduction, the way the police chief had investigated it, how interest had waned after a short time and he'd still kept the case open, hoping for a break.

"Mr. and Mrs. Clark hired a private investigator," Halle said. "Do you recall his name or the names if there was more than one?"

"They did talk to Doc Boone. I don't know what came of the visit. The Clarks never mentioned it again." Luther scratched at his chin. "The trouble is Doc Boone died a few years back. But his daughter, Jessie, took over the business. She probably has his files. She's a year or two younger than you, Halle, so I don't know how much she'll recall from the case. Don't hurt to ask, either way."

"It does not," Halle said. She stood. "Thank you so much for helping us out, Luther."

Liam stood, as well.

"Happy to." The former chief pushed to his feet.

"If you recall anything that might be useful, please let me know. Chief Brannigan gave you my number, I believe."

"He did, and I assure you I will."

Liam and the other man regarded each other a moment but neither said anything.

When they were in the truck once more, Liam asked, "We going to see this Jessie Boone now?"

"We are."

Liam had changed his flight for one on Monday. He wasn't sure staying that long was a good idea but it was done now. Might as well make the most of his time here. Prove to these people that he had nothing to hide. And prove to himself that he had always been Liam Hart.

THE BOONE AGENCY was off the square by one street. Luckily for them the office was open and Jessie Boone was willing to talk.

"Daddy always said that was the worst case of his career," Jessie said.

She was an attractive lady. Blond hair done up in one of those big hairdos. Her clothes were skin-tight. She had that sort of brassy, sexy vibe down to a science, and while Liam admired her style, she wasn't his type.

"It was a tragedy," Halle agreed.

"I'm happy to pull the case file and show you my daddy's notes," she offered, "but I can tell you now there's nothing there. Luther called and asked me to help y'all out if I could, so I had a look to refresh my memory. Daddy wasn't one to take people's money. He only worked on the case a few days and when he didn't pick up a trail he told the Clarks he wasn't the man they needed."

"Do you recall or did your father perhaps annotate who they went to next?"

"He sure did." Jessie nodded. "Daddy recommended they go to Buster Dean over in Tullahoma. He had a bigger operation than Daddy's. Back then he had about four fellas working for him. I don't know about now. But he's the man you need to talk to."

Halle thanked the lady and they left the same way they had arrived.

Empty-handed.

Chapter Eight

NOW

Tullahoma

Before driving to Tullahoma, Halle exchanged her
dad's truck for her car. She was more comfortable
in her vehicle and had only used her father's for the
rough ride to Holcomb's place. Once parked at their
destination, she and Liam climbed out and walked
around the corner to the PI's business address.

Buster Dean's office was situated on West Lincoln Street next to London's Bar and Grill on the
corner at North Wall Street. Halle had never had
any reason to visit the PI's office, but she had eaten
at London's numerous times.

Dean's office was closed. No surprise. It was
well after normal business hours. Still, it was dis-
appointing.

"I guess we can try finding his home address

and see if he's there," she suggested and pulled out her phone to go to an address search website. No luck. A PI would know how to keep his personal info private.

"Nothing," she said to Liam. She nodded toward the restaurant. "Maybe someone next door will know him well enough to have his home address." She started toward London's. The trouble was, that person might not be willing to give out the info.

Only one way to find out.

London's was already packed. It was Friday night, after all. The vintage venue was chock-full of charm with its wood floors and exposed brick walls. A waitress, young, brunette and dressed like a model, approached and asked how many in their party for seating purposes. She glanced at Halle but her gaze settled on Liam and stayed there.

"Actually," Halle said drawing the other woman's attention from Liam, "I'm trying to locate Mr. Dean. His office is already closed and it's urgent that I see him. Do you think your manager might know his cell phone number or his home address? I'm a reporter and we're doing a story on his legendary history in the world of private investigations."

The woman blinked once, twice. "I'll ask her."

She turned and disappeared into the dimly lit sea of tables.

"Did you learn to improvise like that in reporter school?"

Halle met his wary gaze. "I learned that long before, but I've honed the skill over the years."

His eyes narrowed, telegraphing his suspicion and impatience.

"Don't worry, I would never improvise with the important stuff. Everything I've told you and shown you is the truth to the best of my knowledge."

He looked skeptical still, but he said nothing.

The waitress returned with another woman, this one older and far more harried-looking. She wore black slacks with a white boyfriend-style shirt, the collar turned up. Her dangly silver earrings bounced against the white cotton. "I'm Kelly Kessler, the manager tonight," she said. "How can I help you?"

Halle restated her improvised mission, infusing as much excitement into her tone as possible. She even added, "I understand London's is one of his favorite hangouts."

The woman grinned. "For more than forty years now."

"Great," Halle enthused. "That's the kind of detail that will be perfect for my piece." She frowned then. "Unfortunately, I didn't make it down from Nashville in time to catch him in the office. It was supposed to be a surprise that he'd been chosen for the feature. Now I'm not sure I'll be able to find him and I have to submit the story early on Sunday morning."

"Oh, well, we can't have Buster missing out on this chance." She removed a card from her bosom and the pen from behind her ear and started to scribble. "I'll give you his cell number and his home address. This card has my number on it, so if you have any trouble, call me and I'll track him down."

She offered the card to Halle. "Thank you. I will absolutely call you for some more shout-out lines." She looked around. "This is a great place."

Beaming, the woman nodded. "Happy to help."

Halle thanked her and returned to the car. When they'd climbed in, she called the cell number and the call promptly went to voice mail. "Motlow Road it is," she announced, starting the car. She would not be defeated just yet.

Highway 55 led out of Tullahoma proper and it only took a few minutes to reach Motlow Road. Tullahoma was a nice town. Home to Motlow College and boasting its share of historic sites, golfing, boating and even a few tourist attractions like the George A. Dickel & Company Whiskey Distillery.

"Have you heard of this PI?" Liam wanted to know.

"I've heard the name over the years, generally related to some court case. Dean has been around the block a number of times. My father could probably tell us more about him. He falls into the category of men who people don't fully trust but they go to him when they need the kind of help only he can provide. But I've been gone for a while, so his reputation might be different now."

"Do you plan to stay? In the area?"

She glanced at him; he was watching her. Had been. She'd felt his gaze on her. "I don't know yet. Maybe. My parents are getting older and I'm all they've got." She shrugged. "I've always thought about writing a novel. My job here would allow plenty of time for that."

"Like your Aunt Daisy?"

Halle smiled. Surprised that he remembered. "Sort of, but I think I'd prefer true crime."

"What?" he asked. "You don't believe in romance? One failed marriage and you're ready to throw in the towel?"

Now, there was a tough question—two actually. "I do believe in romance. I look at my parents and I can't not believe in romance. It's basic. In our genetic makeup. But my writing interests run more to the kind of reporting I've done in recent years. Homicides. Missing persons. That sort of thing."

"So this is just another story for you."

She slowed for the turn onto Motlow Road. "No." She glanced at him again. "Not at all. This is about finding the truth. This is about a part of *my* life."

He didn't say more. Good thing. Halle needed to focus on the house numbers that were listed on the mailboxes. The houses were set too far back from the road for the numbers to be visible on the home's front door.

Buster Dean lived in a midcentury modern sort of farmhouse with all the typical architectural lines of the era but with board and batten siding and a metal roof. There was a barn and fencing for horses and, from the looks of the property, a good number of acres.

Halle hoped there were no dogs that might bite strangers.

She got out of the car. Liam did the same. Silence crowded in around them. No barking dog, thankfully. No sound of work being done somewhere on the property. Just the peace and quiet of country living. No one was around. Not what Halle had hoped for.

They crossed the yard uneventfully. A half dozen or so hard knocks on the front door and the silence still echoed in the air. No sound inside, either; at least none she could hear.

"Maybe he's out with friends," Liam commented. "Or on a case."

"Apparently. I'll try his cell again later." She surveyed the yard. "For now, it's back to Winchester, I guess."

More of that silence followed them out of the driveway and back to Winchester. Twenty minutes of no words, just the occasional sigh, mostly from her, and a little traffic noise as they maneuvered through evening commuters. She was glad there were no reporters holding vigil outside her house or the Clarks'.

When they had pulled into her drive, he said, "Maybe I should get my rental car out of the Clarks' driveway."

"No rush. It's probably a good thing that it's there. People will think someone is home."

He didn't argue. Instead he followed her up to her apartment.

"Several of the restaurants in town deliver. What's your preference? American? Chinese? More Mexican?"

"You pick," he said.

"Chinese it is, then."

Halle left her bag on the sofa and made the call. When she tossed her cell onto the coffee table, she said, "Forty minutes."

He looked around as if uncertain what to do next.

"Have a seat and we'll hash out what we learned today."

"Did we learn something?" He dropped onto the sofa.

She joined him, with an entire cushion between them. "We learned—" she picked up her cell and opened the photos app "—that Nancy Clark believed you to be her missing son." She passed him the phone with the photos she had snapped during their search of the boxes in Nancy's bedroom.

He swiped through the photos of him from various times in his life, his expression unreadable. "I don't know why she had someone watching me," he finally said. "I am not Andy." He passed the phone back to Halle.

Her shoulders slumped. "How can you still dismiss the idea? These photos are you. They were taken by a woman whose son looked exactly like you in his childhood photos. One coincidence I could buy, but two? As a child, you could have been Andy's twin. You had a dog—an identical dog—named Sparky. Come on. She probably sent you that newspaper because somehow she knew who you were."

"You can't be certain she sent it," he argued.

"You know she did. It's the only reasonable explanation."

"There is nothing reasonable about this, Halle." His jaw had gone rigid, blue eyes icy with tension. "Don't you think I would remember if I was abducted when I was seven years old? It doesn't make any sense. What are you going to suggest next? That my father did some sort of brainwashing technique?"

"I've done my research, Liam," she said calmly. She wasn't some rookie or a fool. "Most memories up to the age of seven are forgotten. The few that linger beyond that age are hardly ever reflective of reality. They've been reshaped into something that fits whatever your life is at that point. So the answer is no. Particularly with a little coaching, you likely wouldn't remember your childhood here if you were removed from it for the rest of your life."

"Come on. You're saying I was taken and suddenly I stopped being Andy Clark and started being Liam Hart? Give me a break."

"Of course I'm not saying that. It would take time and work. But you have mentioned plenty of memo-

"One Minute" Survey

You get TWO books and TWO Mystery Gifts...

ABSOLUTELY FREE!

YOU pick your books – WE pay for everything!

See inside for details.

Dear Reader,

Your opinions are important to us. So if you'll participate in our fast and free "One Minute" Survey, **YOU** can pick two wonderful books that **WE** pay for!

As a leading publisher of women's fiction, we'd love to hear from you. That's why we promise to reward you for completing our survey.

IMPORTANT: Please complete the survey and return it. We'll send your Free Books and Free Mystery Gifts right away. **And we pay for shipping and handling too!**

We pay for
EVERYTHING!

Thank you again for participating in our "One Minute" Survey. It really takes just a minute (or less) to complete the survey... and your free books and gifts will be well worth it!

Sincerely,

Pam Powers

Pam Powers
for Reader Service

"One Minute" Survey

GET YOUR FREE BOOKS AND FREE GIFTS!

✓ Complete this Survey   ✓ Return this survey

▶ DETACH AND MAIL CARD TODAY! ▶

1 Do you try to find time to read every day?

☐ YES   ☐ NO

2 Do you prefer stories with suspenseful storylines?

☐ YES   ☐ NO

3 Do you enjoy having books delivered to your home?

☐ YES   ☐ NO

4 Do you find a Larger Print size easier on your eyes?

☐ YES   ☐ NO

YES! I have completed the above "One Minute" Survey. Please send me my Two Free Books and Two Free Mystery Gifts (worth over $20 retail). I understand that I am under no obligation to buy anything, as explained on the back of this card.

❏ I prefer the regular-print edition
182/382 HDL GNSS

❏ I prefer the larger-print edition
199/399 HDL GNSS

FIRST NAME	LAST NAME

ADDRESS

APT.#	CITY

STATE/PROV.	ZIP/POSTAL CODE

READER SERVICE—Here's how it works:

ries of when you were eight. By then you were set-tled in, fully convinced home was where you were."

He shook his head. "I can't buy it."

"Will you believe DNA? You did say you'd will-ingly leave a sample for the test."

"Sure. Why not? The sooner I can put this be-hind me, the better."

Halle wished she could save him the wasted ef-fort of pretending. He was Andy Clark. There was no other option.

"I'll call Chief Brannigan and see if he can set it up. That way it's official."

"Great." The sarcasm that accompanied the word made her flinch.

He was tired, frustrated and no doubt confused. Halle gave him grace for those reasons when what she wanted to do was shake him.

LIAM WAS READY TO RUN outside and down the stairs to yell at the top of his lungs. *My name is Liam Hart. I am not Andy Clark.*

Except…there were some things that needed to be cleared up. Like why that poor murdered lady had someone taking pictures of him for her. And why Sparky used to be Andy Clark's dog. Or at least a dog that looked exactly like Sparky.

Jesus Christ, he felt like he was in an episode of *The Twilight Zone.* He kept waiting for someone to wake him up from this crazy dream.

His gaze lit on Halle as she answered the door.

Was the food here already? He blinked and watched as she paid the delivery guy. He should have done that, but he couldn't bring himself to speak up or to even move. He was stuck in this in-between place that felt completely wrong but somehow strangely right.

Some part of him felt a connection to this clever reporter. Maybe it was just plain old desire, considering he had been too busy for a social life—much less a sex life—for a few months now. Maybe it was nothing more than basic nature.

Except it felt like more. In the past twenty-four hours his instincts had drawn him closer and closer to her. He felt like he'd known her his whole life. He refused to tell her as much. Hell, she was already fully convinced that he was this Andy Clark.

But he couldn't be. If he was that would mean his entire life since age seven was a lie. He would not allow her or anyone else to take that from him. He loved his father. Missed him so much. He loved Penelope and Claire. He would not permit anyone to tell him that they weren't really his family.

He couldn't.

His cell vibrated in his pocket. He pulled it from his jacket. *Claire*. He walked to the kitchen area, his back to Halle and the delivery guy and answered. "Hey. Everything okay?"

He had sent his sister a text message today and told her he'd decided to stay a few more days but there hadn't been time to call and discuss his reasons. Now, he supposed, was as good a time as any.

"So why are you not coming home before Monday?"

She sounded curious but he heard no alarm in her voice. Good. "The woman who sent me the article was murdered last night."

"Oh my God, are you kidding?"

"Afraid not. The chief of police wants me to stay a couple days. He thinks she was murdered because I showed up."

"Are you a suspect?"

The alarm was loud and clear now. "No. No. I am not a suspect." He opted not to mention that he'd been cleared of suspicion.

Halle had placed the food on the counter and was looking at him as if she feared there was more bad news.

He turned the phone away and said, "It's Claire, my sister."

Halle nodded.

"Are you with *her*?" Claire asked.

Gone was the alarm and in its place was something like defensiveness or a protectiveness. Was his little sister worried about the big bad reporter? Liam had to smile.

"She's standing right in front of me," he said. "Would you like to speak to her?"

"No! Why would I want to speak to her?"

As his sister ranted on, he whispered to Halle. "She's a little shy."

Halle smiled and he relaxed. Her smile did that to him more often than not. Another of those strange connections between them.

"I called Mom."

Liam stilled. "Why did you do that? She's in Paris on vacation. This will just upset her and she doesn't need that in her life." His frustration spiked again. He had no interest in hurting or worrying Penelope. Not until he knew more, and the path was clearer.

"Because we need answers. She's the only one who might have some. Especially since you said that woman was murdered. Oh my God. This is just awful."

"What did you say to her?" Just how big a deal this was going to turn into with Penelope was what Liam needed to know.

The scents of ginger and sesame and garlic were prodding his appetite. He'd been certain he wasn't hungry until those sweet and spicy smells invaded his olfactory senses.

"I told her about the newspaper article and that you were in Winchester looking into it."

He knew his sister. She'd just given him the condensed version. "And what did she say?"

"Not a lot really. She did a lot of listening and about the time she started to respond, the connection went haywire. All staticky and breaking up. She promised she would call me back but she hasn't yet."

He could only imagine what his stepmother was thinking. She had been a great mom to him, still was. From her perspective she might think he was casting her off in search of a new mother.

"I wish you hadn't done that, Claire." He pressed his forehead to the nearest cabinet door and closed his eyes. "I didn't want her upset by this."

"She didn't sound upset."

He dropped his head back and stared at the ceiling. "You just said the connection was broken and staticky. How do you know she wasn't upset?"

"Because what I did hear sounded brisk and commanding. Her usual tone."

"Okay—" he shook his head "—so she wasn't upset. She's angry. That's so much better." Why did little sisters—even after they were adults—have to be such a pain in the butt?

"Trust me, Liam, she is not upset or angry. She's just considering. You know, processing the information."

"Fine. Fine. Fine." He would hear from Penelope by tomorrow. He was certain of it. Maybe that was good, though. He could explain why he felt compelled to do this.

"When are you coming home? I mean, really."

He loved that her voice told him that she missed him, was worried about him. "Monday."

"Good. Don't delay your flight again. It sounds as if all this trip has done is create more questions than provide answers. I'm sorry I urged you to go."

"You have my word that I will not delay unless I have no other choice."

He frowned at his own words. He almost sounded as if he expected to have to postpone leaving again.

Ridiculous.

"Okay, if I hear from Mom, I'll let you know."

"Don't worry, Claire Bear, everything is under control."

"I always know when you're lying," she warned.

"Good night, Claire."

"Love you!"

"Love you, too." He ended the call and took a deep breath. He liked his life. Which was why he didn't like thinking of it not being real.

His gaze shifted to the woman opening Chinese takeout boxes. But some part of him wanted her in it. How screwed up was that? He barely knew her.

She turned to him as if he'd said the words out loud. "You call your sister Claire Bear?"

He smiled at the memory of his little sister as a baby. "She growled when she was a baby. I started calling her a bear and it stuck."

Halle's eyes were bright as if she were about to cry. Had he said something wrong? Reminded her of some memory that made her sad? Oh wait, just looking at him made her sad because he looked exactly like her long-lost childhood friend. How could he forget?

"That's what I called Andy. Andy Bear. Because he was like a life-size, cuddly teddy bear."

Liam pressed his hand to his gut and went for a subject change. "Man, I'm hungry."

She blinked and turned away. "Well, let's eat, then. When we're done, we have a lot of talking to do. Details to go over."

He nodded. "Yes, ma'am. You're the boss."

She looked at him and he realized his mistake.

Andy always let her be the boss.

THEN

August 1
Twenty-six years, eight months ago...

"I CAN'T BELIEVE school starts in two weeks." Halle wasn't ready for second grade. She really, really wasn't. Her mom had bought her all those new clothes and shoes and still she was really freaked out about second grade.

"It's no big deal," Andy assured her. "It'll be just like first grade except we already know how to read. We'll learn lots of new stuff. Harder math and junk like that. It'll be easy as pie, as my dad says."

Halle groaned and rolled to her side to look at her best friend in the whole world. "I don't know about that harder math stuff. I'm not so good at it. Remember in first grade how I had a bumpy start. Ms. Gardner said so."

He stopped counting stars in the sky and turned

his face to hers. "I'll help you. Just like in first grade. Don't worry."

She smiled. He was right. He had helped her past that bumpy start. "'Kay."

She relaxed onto her back and stared up at the dark sky and tried to find where she'd left off counting. Not possible. Ugh. They were lying on a quilt in her backyard. It was nearly bedtime. Would be bedtime already if school had started. But their moms let them stay up a little later in the summer to do fun stuff after dark. Like catching lightning bugs and counting stars.

"What if we're not in the same room together," Halle dared to whisper. She had crossed her fingers every night as she went to sleep, hoping and praying that she and Andy would be in the same room again this year.

"My mom said we will be in the same room," Andy assured her. "She spoke to the principal or something." He rolled his head to the side and grinned at her. "She said your mom did, too."

Halle made a pretend mad face. "She didn't tell me. All this time she's been saying, we'll see. We'll see." She said her mom's words in a silly-stern voice.

Andy laughed. "Even if we weren't in the same room we would still be best friends. Right?"

"Right." She turned back to the stars and silently repeated the words she'd said every night all summer:

Star light, star bright,

The first star I see tonight;

I wish I may, I wish I might,
Have the wish I wish tonight.
I wish to always be with Andy.

Chapter Nine

NOW

Saturday, March 14

Liam was surprised that he didn't hear from Penelope. Maybe she was too angry or hurt at his actions to call. He didn't blame her. She had gone above and beyond to treat him as much like her own child as she did Claire. He didn't want her to see this as some sort of betrayal to her or to his father.

He sat in his rental car across the street from the Lane and Clark homes.

Halle had asked him to be here by nine. It was eight forty-five now. He'd arrived a few minutes early just to think.

Two news vans still loitered on the street but the chief of police had warned them not to park in front of the Clark or Lane homes. A police cruiser went past every couple of hours. Liam had seen it go through five or so minutes after he had arrived.

Most of last night had been spent tossing and turning. His dreams had thrown him back and forth between this life—the one Halle had told him about—and the one he'd always believed to be his.

He studied the house where Andy Clark had lived. He imagined the boy playing in the yard, chasing after his dog named Sparky. Climbing that big oak. Liam shook his head. How was this possible? Instincts he wanted to deny hummed, warning that there was more to this than he wanted to see. Halle Lane felt as familiar to him as anyone he had known his whole life and yet they had only met the day before yesterday.

Before he could stop himself he was climbing out of the rental car. He strode across the street to the Clark home. Yellow crime scene tape flapped in the breeze, slapping against the front porch railing. He walked all the way around to the back porch and sat down on the steps. He stared out over the lawn, then closed his eyes. In his mind he could see the basketball hoop that used to be attached to the side of the garage. He opened his eyes. It wasn't there but he somehow knew it once was.

He shook his head at the foolishness of playing this game with himself. Yet, he closed his eyes again and looked backward. Back to a different time. He saw his dog Sparky, his tongue hanging out as he bounded around, wanting to play chase or ball. A memory of Sparky digging ferociously in one of the flower beds had his eyes opening again.

He walked back to the flower bed he'd seen in the memory, real or imagined, beneath the dogwood tree and considered it for a time. He needed a shovel.

Before second thoughts could stop him, he strode to the picket fence that separated the yards, hopped over it and kept walking until he reached the Lanes' garage. Halle exited her door and looked down at him from the landing.

"I was about to come looking for you."

He frowned. "Is it nine already?"

"Ten after." She started down the stairs, her bag slung over her shoulder, one of those thermal cups likely filled with water or coffee in her hand.

He ignored the idea that he'd been daydreaming in that backyard for nearly half an hour. "I need a shovel." He said this before his brain could catch up with his emotions.

He shouldn't be doing this…shouldn't encourage her delusions.

Except that he was the one having delusions now.

"Okay." She descended the final step. "My dad has all sorts of garden tools in there." She gestured to the walk-through door that led into the garage at the bottom of the stairs.

He went inside, turned on a light and located a small shovel. He didn't want to damage the flowers, so small would work best.

Shovel in hand, he turned off the light, pulled the door shut and walked back to the fence, hung a leg over and then the other one. At the dogwood tree, he walked around it once, then selected a spot and started to dig. Halle moved up beside him and watched while he nudged around between the roots. This was a really old, really big—for a dogwood—tree.

He found nothing. He moved over a foot or so, spread apart the daffodils sprouting from the soil and mulch and started to dig once more.

"Can I ask what you're looking for?"

"I don't know." The tip of the shovel hit something hard.

He scraped back more of the dirt with the shovel, careful not to damage whatever he was about to unearth. Something metal and shiny glinted as he scratched against it.

"It's the time capsule!" Halle crouched down. "Andy never told me where he buried it. He was supposed to, but then…"

"He didn't come back."

Liam stared at the metal object. It was shaped like a thermos, silver or stainless steel, something along those lines.

He squatted next to Halle as she pulled the time capsule from the ground. She swiped the dirt from it and gave the top a twist.

She grunted. "I can't budge it."

She offered it to Liam and he stared at it for a long while before taking it into his hands. The canister felt cold against his palms. He gripped the length of it with his left and grasped the top with his right. It took a couple of tries but the lid twisted open.

He couldn't look inside. His heart was pounding and a cold sweat had formed on his skin. He gave the thermos-like object back to Halle.

She placed the lid on the ground at her feet and used two fingers to reach inside. The first item she withdrew was a photo. Andy and Halle with their bicycles, his was blue, hers was red.

She laughed. "I wanted a big bicycle so badly. I warned my mother that when she bought me one it better not be pink. Pink was for sissies."

Liam stared at the photo and in his mind it seemed to come to life, like those live photos he took with his cell. This was what he saw: he could hear Halle laughing. Watched his big grin as he burst into laughter, too.

"What were you laughing about?"

She stared at him—he didn't need to look, he felt her eyes on him. Then he realized what he'd done.

"We," she said pointedly, "were laughing at the idea that since we had big kid bikes we could see the world."

He passed the photo back to her. His gut clenched hard and more sweat oozed onto his skin.

She reached into the capsule again and this time she pulled out a folded page and something else fell out with it. He picked up the dried four-leaf clover that had fallen to the cold ground. Instantly images of the two of them on their hands and knees, combing through the grass, whispered through his mind. He blinked them away. This—all of this—was putting ideas in his head. The memory couldn't be his. It was hers...and Andy's.

She held the piece of paper and tears slid down her cheeks.

He closed his eyes and banished the feelings that surged. *Not real. Not me. Not possible.*

"Dear Halle, we're probably old now," she recited. "But whatever we are and wherever we are, we'll still be friends. Your best friend, Andy. PS: my mom helped me spell all the words right."

She swiped her eyes and tucked the letter and the photo back into the tube. Liam dropped the four-leaf clover inside.

"We should—" she cleared her throat "—straighten this up and head out to Tullahoma. That PI called me back. He said we could come by his house. Let me go wash my hands."

Liam grabbed the shovel and pushed the dirt into the now empty hole as Halle went back to her apartment, taking the time capsule with her. By the time he'd stowed the shovel back into the garage and washed up at the sink there, she'd descended the stairs. Hands empty and clean.

She nodded and led the way to her car. They climbed in and she put the car in Reverse and started to roll down the drive. Her mom waved from the kitchen window. Halle waved back and Liam did, as well. Mrs. Lane's face was suddenly replaced by the young face of Nancy Clark. She waved and smiled and his heart thumped.

Liam closed his eyes, shook his head to clear the image.

"Did you have breakfast?"

"Yeah." When she had backed onto the street he dared to open his eyes again. "You?"

"Are you kidding? My mother insists I come to her kitchen and have breakfast with her and Dad every morning. Then I hurry back to my place and brush away the smell of bacon and grits and seriously strong coffee."

No matter that his brain felt bruised from all the bouncing back and forth from the past to the present, he laughed. "That sounds way better than my extra dry muffin and fake OJ."

"You should have breakfast with us tomorrow," she suggested. "Mom and Dad would love it. Plus, if you're leaving on Monday it will be an opportunity to say goodbye."

"I am leaving on Monday." That pounding started in his chest again. He took a deeper breath and ordered himself to calm.

"How did you know about the time capsule?"

For about three seconds he considered not answering. He'd had enough questions. The answers were even worse than the questions. He didn't want to do this.

"I didn't know. I just felt the need to dig around those flowers. It was…"

He didn't know what it was.

When she didn't respond he added, "I remembered Sparky digging at those same kinds of flowers. Maybe that's why I did. We have flowers like that back home."

"You had a memory of being in that yard."

Damn it. "The power of suggestion is a formidable force. That's why when there are multiple witnesses to a crime, the first thing the police do is separate them. If one witness hears the other's story, there's a good chance the second witness will mold his or her story to that of the first witness."

"True," she agreed. "But I didn't mention anything about a time capsule. I'd forgotten."

"You mentioned the dog." The words came out harsher than he'd intended. He pressed his head against the seat. He didn't want to think right now. He felt confused and rattled and in way over his head.

"I did mention the dog." She sighed. "I'm not trying to convince you, Liam. I'm really not. It's best if the evidence convinces you. I think that's happening and the evidence is prompting memories. Not me."

But she was wrong. So wrong. It was her. Her crazy red hair. Those green eyes. All those cute little freckles she didn't even bother to try and hide. It was the sound of her voice. The tinkling of her laughter.

It was everything about her.

THE DRIVE TO Tullahoma was as somber as a wake. Halle wished there was something she could say that would make him feel better but there were no words. This was real and he had to get right with it.

Understanding his reluctance was easy. He had a childhood and parents who loved him. He had a sister, a home. Memories. He didn't want those things to suddenly be wrong, and to suggest that one or both of his parents in California had somehow been involved in his abduction was the only way to make sense of the truth she'd thrust in front of him.

This truth was unpalatable. It called into question who and what he had thought he was. She wished there was a way to do this differently. To make the transition easier or smoother.

But there wasn't an easy slide into this reality.

There was only what they were doing right now.

Halle made the turn off Motlow Road into Mr. Dean's driveway. She rolled all the way to the end, which was quite a distance. He'd told her to come around back since he would be spending the day readying his garden for planting.

She and Liam exited simultaneously and she led the way around back. A German shepherd sat at the garden gate. His ears perked up, eyes keen on the visitors. Halle stalled. Liam did the same.

"Jinx won't bother you, come on in."

The voice came from beyond the weathered wood fence. Liam suddenly stepped in front of her and started forward. He walked past the dog with Halle on his heels. As his master had said, Jinx only watched them pass.

Buster Dean was a large man. At least six-four and 250 pounds. Even at his age, late sixties, Halle surmised, he looked ready to lead the defensive linemen for a pro football team. He was muscular and had the bearing of a man half his age. The only concession to his age was his gray hair.

He propped his garden hoe against the fence and dusted his hands off. "How can I help you folks?"

Halle thrust out her hand. "Mr. Dean, I'm Halle Lane. We spoke on the phone. And this is Liam Hart, my friend."

He shook her hand and then reached for Liam's, gave it a quick shake.

"You mentioned having questions about that lost boy. The one who went missing all those years ago." He glanced at Liam as he said the last.

"Yes, sir. Andy Clark."

"Well—" he scratched his head "—I'm not sure how I can be of any help, but fire away and we'll see what hits a target."

"Mr. Boone in Winchester recommended the Clarks to you when they were looking for a private investigator to help find Andy." Halle held her breath. Couldn't help it. She needed this man to know something that would point them in a helpful direction.

"That's right," he agreed. "Mr. and Mrs. Clark came to me about a month or so after their boy went missing. They were desperate to find him, like any parent would be."

"Were you able to find anything, Mr. Dean?"

He cocked his head and looked at her. "I read the piece you did in the *Gazette*, young lady. If this is for some sort of feature in a Nashville paper, I'd like to know now, seeing as you don't live or work there anymore."

Inwardly, she groaned. She'd been caught. The man was a PI. Of course he did his research. His friend from London's had called him. "I'm hoping this will be a feature. Maybe even a book one day."

She felt Liam's gaze on her.

"The truth is," she said quickly, "it doesn't matter whether it's another article or a book, I—we want to know what happened to Andy Clark. He was my friend, my best friend."

Dean heaved a big breath. "I found nothing. It's the only case in my entire career that left me stumped. The trail was as cold as ice. Whoever took that boy was careful. Meticulous. There wasn't a single mistake. A lot of painstakingly thorough planning went into that abduction."

"Did the Clarks give up at that point?" This was not what she had wanted to hear.

"I don't think so. The two didn't strike me as the type to give up. They wanted to find their boy. Mr. Clark mentioned a lawyer up in Nashville they'd spoken to about adoption. Evidently they'd had problems having a child of their own and were thinking about adoption at some earlier point in their lives. Suddenly she was having a baby and that was that.

But she said this lawyer had a PI and they wondered if I knew anything about him. I figured they were willing to pay top dollar on another man, but I really didn't see anyone turning up anything new."

"Do you remember his name or perhaps you made a note of him in your file on the Clarks?" Halle needed to know in case the Clarks had contacted him.

"I don't know who the PI was, but the lawyer was David Burke. He's the one with those billboards all over the place and the annoying commercials."

Halle knew the one. The jingle that played with every commercial was one of those things that stuck in your head. "Thank you, Mr. Dean." She pulled a card from her bag and handed it to him. "I hope you'll call me if you think of anything else that might help us in our search for the truth."

He looked over her card and nodded. "Be happy to. Y'all be careful out there, now. Some of the folks in my profession don't like to discuss their clients or their cases. They can take offense at anyone showing curiosity. Caution should be your watchword."

Halle thanked him again, then she and Liam walked back to her car. She'd hoped seeing the man in person would stir some memories or unearth more info than a phone call, but they still had little to go on.

When she had settled behind the wheel and he was in the passenger seat, she asked, "You up for a trip to Nashville?"

"Sure." He looked at her as she turned around and headed away from the PI's house. "If you would like, I can drive. I feel kind of useless being chauffeured around."

"Actually—" she flashed him a smile, thankful that the tension he'd felt since finding that time capsule seemed to be diminishing "—that would be great. I'll stop at a gas station before we hit Interstate 24 and you can take over."

"Sounds good."

"THIS IS IT," Halle announced as Liam slowed for a turn into the driveway of the Jackson Boulevard home. To her surprise the security gates were wide open.

The driveway rolled through the manicured trees and circled in front of the house, which was a grand three-story Southern antebellum mansion. Liam parked in front of the house on the cobblestone parking pad.

"This is where the rich people in Nashville live?" Liam asked as he surveyed the massive house and endless landscaping.

"Belle Meade. One of the neighborhoods where the rich live richly." She grinned. "Let's see if Mr. Burke is taking visitors."

They emerged from her sedan that looked completely out of place sitting so close to this multimillion-dollar home. On the way here, since

Liam had driven and wasn't in the mood to talk, she had spent the time doing a little research on Burke.

He'd been married three times, had children with two of the wives. His children were grown and living all over the world according to Google. His last wife had divorced him, citing irreconcilable differences. Halle stared up at the towering mansion. Why would a single man want to live like this? The house had to be twenty thousand square feet.

But then David Burke was incredibly rich. At sixty-seven he had spent the first thirty years of his career taking all sorts of cases and pushing to win bigger settlements. At some point during the latter part of those first thirty years he'd found his formula apparently. He was suddenly one of the richest men in the southeast and was on every who's who list in the state. He still took the high-profile cases, but now people respected those silly commercials and repetitive billboards. After all, Burke was practically a celebrity.

Halle pressed the button for the doorbell. Traditional chimes echoed through the entry hall and good God, what an entry hall! She could see it through the windows on either side of the door. Marble floors and a sweeping, open-style staircase that rose up to the third floor, pristine white banisters overlooking the entry below. Select pieces of no-doubt priceless art hung on the walls. A chair and a bench were placed just so. And in the middle of it all was a beautiful fountain much like one you would see in a lavish mall. She wondered if the bottom would be littered with coins.

As they watched, the man himself strode to the door. Burke looked exactly like the photographs on the internet. Medium height, medium build. Dark hair that was fringed with gray. Ordinary. If you passed him on the street you would never know he lived in a house such as this unless you recognized the designer label that stated loudly and clearly that his suit cost a small fortune all on its own.

He opened the door, looked surprised. Apparently he'd been expecting someone else. "Who are you?" he asked, looking from one to the other. Then he held up a hand. "Please. I don't go to church and I have no interest in learning about your beliefs." He reached into his right trouser pocket. "If it's a donation you're looking for—"

"Mr. Burke," Halle interrupted, "my name is Halle Lane and this is Liam Hart. We're here to discuss the Clark case with you."

His gaze lingered on Liam. Halle wasn't sure if he thought he recognized him or if he was simply interested more in Liam than Halle.

"Clark case?" He shifted his attention to Halle. "Are you referring to the boy who disappeared all those years ago? I saw something in the paper recently about that case."

Halle decided not to point out to him that it was her story he'd seen. Every newspaper in Nashville had picked it up.

"Yes, that's the one. I'm a friend of the family and Mrs. Clark recently passed away. In settling her estate and going through some of her papers, there was a reference to you. I thought perhaps you could shed some light on what sort of help you provided the Clark family." She'd come up with that cover on the way here, as well. It wasn't entirely untruthful. Her mother would be settling the Clark estate and they had been going through her papers.

"Yes. I recall now. Why don't you come inside out of the chill?"

It was a little crisp this morning. "Thank you."

Halle followed him inside and Liam stayed close behind her. Burke led them across the foyer that extended from the front of the house to the back, and to the right into a large great room or family room. There were two huge televisions hanging on the walls and a sofa large enough for a party of twenty. The sofa was a sectional, like hers, only leather and about five times larger. The view out the floor-to-ceiling windows was of more lush landscape and an enormous pool.

"Can I offer you a drink?" Burke held out his hands. "Water, coffee, something stronger? Scotch? A martini?"

"No, thank you," Halle declined.

Liam shook his head, declining also.

"In that case, let's get to the point. As we say in my line of work, time is money—even on Saturday.

I have a client coming, which is who I thought you were." He gestured to the sofa. "Please, sit."

Halle lowered to the edge of the sofa. Liam sat beside her while Burke took a seat across the coffee table from the two of them.

"The Clarks came to me when they still lived in Nashville. I don't know, maybe thirty-three or thirty-four years ago."

"They wanted to adopt," Halle suggested. Mr. Dean had mentioned as much.

"Yes. You may or may not be aware but at the time older couples had a strike against them when it came to adoption. There were questions like potential health issues that might come into play during the adopted child's early years. The Clarks had run into a bit of that sort of thing and decided to try for a private adoption. Their finances were more than adequate to consider going that route, so they came to me. I had already forged quite a reputation. My name had become nearly synonymous with private adoptions."

"But they didn't go through with an adoption," Halle said, recalling the rest of what Mr. Dean had said.

"That's correct. Mrs. Clark learned she was pregnant and they decided not to pursue the adoption."

"When did they come to you next?" Liam asked, speaking for the first time.

Halle was startled that he had but she was glad. He was part of this; he should speak up.

"Maybe two months after their little boy went missing." Burke made a sad face. "It was such a tragedy. The rip-your-guts out kind of devastation."

"Were they planning to try adopting again?" Liam asked.

"No, no. They wanted my help with finding him. The police were coming up empty-handed and they thought I might be able to help. I have quite a team of investigators at my disposal. They had met the investigator who checked out all the birth parents for the adoptions I handled. I suppose they were impressed by his work and thought he might be able to help them find their son."

"Was he able to help them?" Halle asked.

"No, sadly not," Burke said. "I think that news was like a stake through the heart for the already desolate couple." He shook his head. "I wish I could have done more."

"We'd like to speak to this investigator," Liam said.

Halle was impressed. He was learning the tricks of her trade. "Being able to speak to him would be immensely useful," she tacked on.

"Unfortunately, he no longer works for me. In fact, we lost touch about seven or eight years ago. He opened his own shop. I think the emotions involved with the adoption process started to get to him."

"If you could give us his name, we'll pay him a visit and see if he can help us," Halle prodded.

"I can't tell you how important this is, even now, twenty-five years later."

Burke's brow furrowed for a moment, then he raised his eyebrows. "Well, of course." He smiled kindly, ever the showman. "I can even tell you where his office is unless he's moved recently."

"Thank you, that would be very helpful." Halle pulled out her cell and readied to enter the information into her notes.

"Frank Austen with an *e*. His office is—or was—on Nolensville Pike." He provided the street number. Didn't have his new cell number. It had apparently changed since he worked for Burke.

"Thank you, Mr. Burke." Halle stood. "We really appreciate your help."

"Certainly." He smiled that megawatt smile he used in his commercials and on his billboards.

He walked to the front door with them. Once they were across the threshold Halle hesitated. "You wouldn't happen to have his home address? Since it's Saturday we might not be able to catch him at the office."

"I can tell you where he once lived, but I have no idea if he's still there."

"That's a starting place," Halle urged.

Burke provided the street address and Halle thanked him again.

When they reached the car, Liam said, "Why don't you drive? You know your way around downtown Nashville."

"Sure."

When they were driving away, Liam spoke again. "He watched us leave before going back into the house."

"He probably doesn't have people show up unannounced at his private residence very often."

"I got a bad vibe from that guy."

Halle glanced at him before pulling onto the road that would take them back into Nashville proper. "I noticed he was checking you out when we first arrived."

"No, not that kind of vibe. The kind that tells me he's not a nice guy."

This was more true than he knew. Halle had found considerably more in her research than all the success stories about Burke. There were rumors he was in trouble with the IRS and he'd been sanctioned by the court on more than one occasion.

But if the name he'd given them could help find what they needed, Halle would be grateful.

Chapter Ten

NOW

Frank Austen's office was closed and he wasn't at home. No surprise there, Liam decided. He wasn't sure what they could expect on a Saturday. They had gotten lucky with the lawyer, Burke. If he hadn't been expecting a client, he probably wouldn't have been home and they would never have made it past his gate.

Liam would have expected a celebrity—a notorious one might be a better term according to all that Halle had told him—to have private security on site at his home. Maybe he'd given them the day off in deference to his expected appointment. Or maybe his security staff had been monitoring the meeting and would have appeared if needed.

Sometimes it was all about the appearance. He had a feeling David Burke liked to come off as relaxed and in control at all times. But no one was that good. Everyone made mistakes, kept secrets.

Even his parents, apparently.

He wanted to believe none of this was possible but every minute of each day he was with Halle, he understood it was more than just possible.

This was real.

But Liam wasn't ready to fully accept that conclusion unconditionally. Not yet anyway. Some tiny part of him still held out a desperate hope that his life was really what he believed it to be and not something else…something sinister and filled with secrets and lies and betrayals.

"I'm taking you to lunch at my all-time favorite place," Halle announced. She shot him a questioning look. "If that's okay with you?"

He shrugged. "Sure. There's not much I won't eat."

She flashed him a smile. "Good. I like a guy who isn't afraid to be adventurous."

Just when he'd thought nothing could make him smile. "Good to know."

They shared a look and warmth spread through him. He knew that gaze: it was as familiar as his own reflection.

He decided to relax and enjoy the urban landscape as she drove. It seemed every time he opened his mouth he said more than he intended or the wrong thing. Or she looked at him a certain way and he suddenly felt that bond that couldn't possibly be real.

Traffic was a bear but Halle knew her way around. If she saw a bottleneck ahead, she changed their route. She was a bold driver. Nothing he hadn't expected. Her personality was bold.

When she parked in front of a seriously low-rent-looking diner, he was a little surprised and a whole lot skeptical. The place wasn't at all what he had expected. The building looked old and even a little run-down, and, frankly, kind of sketchy.

"I promise they have the best burgers in the world."

Liam glanced at her and made an agreeable sound. There wasn't a lot to say. Still, judging by the number of cars parked around the place, there had to be something halfway decent going on inside.

"It's one of the oldest—if not the oldest—places in Nashville," she explained as they got out. "You're as likely to run into a celebrity as anyone else. The atmosphere is totally laid-back."

He nodded, deciding to reserve judgment for now.

Inside she grabbed his hand and led him through the bar area and to the dining room. She waved at a waitress who literally whooped at seeing her. The waitress hurried over and ushered them to a table—the only free one in the room. Classic Formica and metal tables, like from the fifties or sixties.

"I haven't seen you in forever, girl," the woman gushed before giving Halle a big hug. She turned to Liam then. "Who is this gorgeous human?"

Halle laughed. "Melany, this is Liam Hart. Liam, Melany. She's the best waitress in town."

The woman grinned. "That and a good tip will get you everywhere, honey. Now, sit and tell me how you've been."

Halle took a seat, and Liam did the same. While she brought her friend up to speed, he pulled a menu from between the napkin holder and the ketchup bottle and gave it a look.

"You won't need that, sugar." Melany took the menu from him and stuck it back where he'd gotten it. "You want the cheeseburger, fries and a cold draft brew."

"Trust her," Halle said. "It's the best."

Liam gave the lady a nod. "I'm in."

"Great. I'll be back in a flash."

Melany hurried away, waving and saying hello to other customers as she passed.

"The staff is definitely friendly," he noted.

"Always."

As promised, Melany was back with two frosty mugs of beer. "Enjoy!" And then she was off again.

"So you came here often," Liam said as he picked up the mug.

"At least once a week. I lived on Woodmont in Green Hills. It was like six or seven minutes to get here. My ex wasn't so keen on the place, so I didn't come as often as I might have."

"The ex." Liam nodded. "Tell me about the ex."

She blinked, looked a little reluctant but didn't balk. "He was good at his job. Very good. He's still one of the top television producers in Nashville. I was a mere lowly reporter but I was good at my job, too."

He'd seen her list of awards. She was good then and now, if the article on Andy Clark was any indication. "But something went wrong."

"He was busy. Always. He wasn't home a lot. The longer we were married—which wasn't that long— the less time he had for me." She shook her head. "Putting all the blame on him isn't really fair. When we married, I was exactly like him. Work was everything. We were the perfect fit. We grabbed the moments we could and were perfectly happy to let our careers be the priority. And once in a while we even shared the same bed or a meal. He wasn't the one who changed, it was me."

"You wanted the whole package," Liam suggested. "The career, the marriage, kids, house with a white picket fence."

It didn't matter if she answered. He knew this about her. Somehow. The idea was at once exhilarating and oddly terrifying. How could he know her feelings unless all that she alleged were true?

"Yes. I wanted it all. Once I passed thirty, something changed inside me. My biological clock started ticking or whatever. But he didn't feel the same way. He was years away from wanting that sort of commitment. So I left him. Moved back into my old place in Green Hills and waited for him to see the error of his ways. But he didn't. He simply moved on. One day there was a knock on my door and a messenger delivered the divorce papers." She shrugged. "He was never one to waste time on a project he didn't feel strongly about."

"Are you still in love with him?" Liam wasn't sure why he felt the need to ask the question. It was none of his business but somehow he needed to know.

"No. Sometimes I think I never really was." She sipped her beer. "I was in love with the idea of him. The idea of us, when what I really loved was my work. But something inside me changed and nothing felt right again."

The food arrived and Mclany waited as they checked to see that all was to their liking. Liam took a big bite of his burger and moaned. Halle and Melany were correct. The burger was fantastic. He told Melany as much and she beamed.

When the waitress had moved away, Halle patted her lips with her napkin and then said, "Told you so."

For a few minutes they focused on devouring their food. The burgers were juicy and tasty. Liam was reasonably certain he'd never had better. Even the fries were damned good. The icy cold beer was the icing on the cake.

"Now it's my turn," she announced when she'd finished off her burger.

"You still have fries on your plate," he pointed out. He picked up the last one of his and popped it into his mouth.

"Don't try and change the subject."

He made a confused face. "How could I do that?

I don't even know what the subject is." This was not exactly true. She wanted to ask him questions about his social life. Quid pro quo.

"Tell me why you haven't married."

"I guess I was like you. Focused on my work. My dad passed and it felt like I needed to do even more. Claire is always telling me I work too hard. But she's the same way. Penelope—my stepmother—has just been sort of lost since he died. She spends as much time away from home as possible."

"What happened to your birth mother?"

"I asked Dad that once and he said they were hiking in the mountains and she fell. When he reached her, she was dead. She may have died instantly but he had to be sure so he climbed down to her with me in tow. Anyway, there was no way he could carry me and her body off that mountain, so he marked the place on the trail and carried me out. When he and the authorities went back, her body was missing. They searched for days but never found her remains. The local wildlife evidently dragged her off to their cave or den."

"I'm so sorry. That must have been truly horrible for your father and you."

"I really don't remember anything about it but it was tough for him. He never liked talking about her death. He would talk about her life, but not the end."

"Completely understandable." Halle shook her head and traced her finger around her sweating glass for a moment before asking her next question. "No girlfriend back home?"

"No." He downed the last of his beer. "No girlfriend."

"There's never been anyone special? Someone you considered spending the rest of your life with?"

"No. The past year was really the first time I considered the idea of what happens next. I don't know if it was a delayed reaction to my father's death or if it was just that biological clock thing for guys." He grinned. "Whatever happens next, I haven't figured it out yet."

"When we were kids—" she stopped. "When I was a kid," she amended, "Andy and I used to talk about the future. He wanted to be a policeman or a fireman. A hero." She smiled. "He loved the idea of helping other people. If things had been different, I'm certain he would have been class president and received all sorts of awards and scholarships. He was so smart and so passionate about life."

Her words brought up more haunting similarities. Liam had never been able to ignore the underdog or those in need. Even Claire had warned him recently that he couldn't give so generously to every charity under the sun. Didn't matter that he'd been class president, either. That was more likely because he was nice to everyone. No reason to mention that ancient history. It would only be another detail she would use as evidence of her claims.

"After you showed up," she said, drawing his attention back to her, "I did some research on you. You do more than your share of giving back, as well. You've been honored by community leaders on several occasions."

"Just following in my dad's footsteps." Luke Hart was a bigger hero than Liam could ever hope to be, which was all the more reason the idea of him stealing a child was simply not plausible.

"Tell me about your father."

Melany showed up to see if they needed another round. Halle ordered water this time. Liam went with her choice.

When the waitress had walked away, Halle looked at him expectantly.

"His name was Luke, Lucas Alexander Hart. He never went to college but insisted that Claire and I did. He started with nothing and somehow managed to talk the bank into lending him the money to buy the vineyard and winery." Liam shook his head. "Whenever he told that story, he always laughed and said it was a miracle they didn't toss him out. But for whatever reasons they gave him the loan and he turned the place into what it was meant to be all along. If he was here, he would also tell you that Penelope was his anchor. Without her he couldn't have managed."

"Sounds like the two of them had a good marriage."

"They did. He always insisted the key was that you had to be friends, too. They were good friends."

The water appeared on the table, along with the check.

"I think he was right," Halle said when the waitress had moved away. "Friendship was missing from my marriage. We were colleagues and lovers but never friends, not really. My parents didn't like him, either, so that was a definite downer. But I think we would have had a far better chance had we been friends, too."

"He was a fool."

She met his gaze, then smiled. "Thank you. I think so, too."

She reached for her bag but he stopped her with a hand on her arm. "It's my turn," he argued as he grabbed the check.

He stopped at the counter and paid on the way out. As they zigzagged through the still crowded lot to reach her car, Halle abruptly stopped.

Liam glanced around. "What's wrong?"

She shrugged. "Maybe nothing. I just had that hair-raising sensation." She laughed. "You know, when it feels like someone is watching you."

He took a moment to slowly scan the street and the parking lot. "I don't see anyone now."

She exhaled a big breath. "Maybe it was my imagination."

He opened her door for her. She stared at him a moment, then said, "Thanks."

He climbed in and fastened his seat belt. There was another question burning in his brain but he waited until she had backed out of the slot and pulled out onto the street before he asked. He hadn't been able to stop thinking about it since they were at Burke's house. "Were you considering writing a book about his disappearance?"

"I'd thought about it, but the time never seemed to be right." She braked for a traffic light. "Some part of me thought maybe if I put all my thoughts and memories into a book, just maybe if he was still alive and out there somewhere, he would read it and remember. He would know we hadn't forgotten him and that we still love him."

He stared at her profile as she moved her foot from the brake to the accelerator and the car rolled forward. The line of her jaw, the rise of her cheekbones, her lips, her nose, all of it filled him with a sudden sense of longing. How would it feel to have someone love you that much? Not a parent or a sibling, but a friend…a lover? His heart started that confounded pounding.

He understood how it would feel. It would feel exactly like this.

Liam looked away. He desperately needed answers. As hard as he tried to keep fighting the possibility that he was, in fact, Andy, that certainty was quickly draining from him.

THE PI, Frank Austen with an *e*, lived in a seriously low-rent neighborhood. The duplex was a box-style brick with no architectural features or interest. Very plain, very flat, save the shallow peak of the roofline. A chain-link fence separated the two halves of the small front yard. A cracked and discolored concrete driveway rolled right up to the door on each side. Like earlier, there was still no vehicle in the driveway. Halle turned in just the same and parked.

"This time if no one comes to the door," she said, "we'll start calling on the neighbors."

"Burke wasn't sure he lived here anymore." Liam opened his door and got out of the car. Across the top, he said, "If he has moved, maybe one of his neighbors will know where."

"We can hope." Halle draped her bag over her shoulder and made the short journey to the front door.

While she knocked without garnering a response, Liam decided to have a look around. He walked to the side of the house, opened the gate that separated the driveway from the backyard. Around back was the same, plain, neglected property, nothing to draw the eye from the drab reddish orange brick or the mostly dead grass. Like the front, the yard was cut in half by the same style chain-link that bordered it. A small concrete patio, five-by-eight or so, bordered each back door. A six-foot wooden privacy fence about eight feet wide had been put up on either side of the chain-link to provide some visual separation from the two patio areas. The patio on this side had a chair and a table. On the table was an

ashtray overrun with cigarette butts. If the PI still
lived here, he was a heavy smoker.

Liam walked to the back door. Gave a knock.
Nothing. No sound inside whatsoever. He tried the
knob but it was locked. From the looks of the knob
it wouldn't take much to open it. He moved on to a
window and cupped his hands to have a look inside.
Yellow-with-age blinds prevented him from seeing
much. Fortunately, several of the louvers were broken, so he managed a glimpse here and there.

"Do you see anything?"

Liam jerked away from the glass. "You couldn't
warn me that you were behind me?"

"I thought about it." She grinned. "But the opportunity to startle you was too good to pass up."

"You've always liked doing that."

Their gazes locked and held for a moment longer,
with him holding his breath at the realization that
came out of nowhere, her looking uncertain what
to say or do next.

"You can't see much inside," he said, moving on,
"but what you can see makes it look as if whoever
lives here is planning a trip or maybe moving."

Halle walked around him and peered through the
window, moving from broken louver to broken louver just as he had.

There was a suitcase on the bed and it was already half filled with men's clothes. The dresser
drawers were pulled out, their remaining contents

hanging haphazardly. The closet doors stood open, many of the hangers now empty.

They moved to the next window, which looked into the kitchen. Dishes were stacked in the sink. An abandoned coffee mug sat on the counter.

"Maybe he's taking a vacation." Halle led the way back around to the front of the house. "Let's go door-to-door and see what the neighbors have to say."

Since the other half of the duplex had a For Rent sign in the window, they moved on to the first neighboring house, the one on the left of the driveway, where a woman with four kids lived. The duplex couldn't have had more than two bedrooms. She had no idea who lived in the house next to her. She quickly closed the door before Halle could ask anything else.

Surveying the street as she moved toward the house on the other side of the duplex, Halle said, "If we don't get anywhere with his residential neighbors, maybe we can find someone next door or across the street from his office. No matter that it's Saturday, there might be someone working around there."

When they'd checked out the guy's office, Liam had spotted one of those check-cashing places that looked open. "It's worth a try."

He wasn't entirely sure what Halle hoped to learn from this PI. But anything he knew might provide insights, he supposed.

Halle knocked on the door of the next house. Dogs barked, shattering the quiet inside. The yaps told him the animals were small ones. Halle knocked again. Someone inside shouted, "Hold your horses." Female, he decided.

A moment passed. Liam suspected the woman inside was having a look through her security peephole. The door opened a crack. "If you're peddling something, I ain't buying."

"Sorry to bother you, ma'am," Halle said. "We're looking for Mr. Frank Austen. He lives next door to you." She gestured to the house next door. "We've been to his office and now here and we can't seem to find him."

The door opened a little wider. The two little dogs she held, one white and one gray, wiggled in her arms. "You probably know he's one of them private investigators," she warned. "They don't like nobody getting in their business."

"Yes, ma'am, I know," Halle agreed. "But it's very important that we find him."

They might be in luck. It sounded as if he still lived here and that this woman knew him.

"He ain't home much," the woman said. "He travels a lot. Does a lot of them stakeouts like on TV. Sometimes we have us a few drinks and talk about it. He's got a lot of stories to tell."

Now Liam got the picture. "Have you and Mr. Austen known each other for a while?" he asked.

"Oh yeah," she said with a wink. "We've been neighbors for thirty years. I watch out for his place when he's out of town and he brings me little gifts from his travels. I like snow globes. I've got a whole room full of them." She narrowed her gaze at Liam. "I know you were back there nosing around behind his house. He won't like that."

"I thought maybe he was out back smoking and didn't hear us. It's really important we find him," Liam urged. "Not to mention I worried he might be ill. It happens. A man without anyone to check on him."

The neighbor shook her head. "Don't nobody ever check on him except me. I don't think he's got no family and he always said if anyone come around it was probably trouble." She looked from Liam to Halle and back. "Are you two trouble?"

"No, ma'am," Halle denied. "We just need to find him. A friend of ours went missing a few years back and I'm hoping he can help us."

"Oh, I hate to hear that. Far as I know, he's in town. I saw him come in yesterday at the butt crack of dawn. I took coffee to him a little later and he looked like hell. He said he'd been up all night on a stakeout. Grumbled about being too old for that stuff anymore. I haven't talked to him since. He left out this morning around eight and he hasn't been back. Since he didn't ask me to get his mail, he's probably coming back tonight or tomorrow. He doesn't like for his mail to sit in the box."

"If I give you my cell number," Halle asked, "will you call me when he comes back home? It really is very important."

"Sure. Let me get a pen and paper." She disappeared into her house.

"He may not be coming back," Liam whispered.

Halle nodded. "That's what I'm worried about."

"Here we go." The lady appeared back at the door with no dogs in tow. She put her pen to the pad she held. "What's your number, hon?"

Halle provided her cell number.

"Do you have his number, by the way? We could try calling him," Halle said.

The woman hesitated, then gave them the number quickly, as if she was unsure whether to share it.

"He don't often answer," she told them. "Just takes the messages and he calls back if wants to."

They thanked her and left. Neither Liam nor Halle spoke again until they were in her car.

As she backed out of the drive, he said, "His packing up could be coincidence?"

Halle looked at him before continuing into the street. "I don't know. He's lived here all these years. His career is here. My article comes out and suddenly this PI who may have done some work for the Clarks twenty-five years ago is packing up to go."

"Wait, wait, wait." Liam held up his hands as she shifted into Drive and started forward. "Are you accusing a man you've never met of some illegal activity more than two decades old? How are you making that leap? You don't even know him."

"It's just…" she said, then shook her head. "I don't know. A feeling. I've had this creepy feeling since we left Burke's house. Something isn't right about him and this Mr. Austen with an *e*."

Liam agreed with her there, for sure.

"Let's try calling him," Halle said, "even if he hardly ever picks up. You remember the number?"

"Etched in my brain." He pulled out his cell, tapped in the digits and waited. Just as the neighbor had predicted, it went to voice mail. He left a message, saying he was a potential client and needed to talk to him about a job.

After he clicked off, he looked at Halle. "Where to now? Do you know anyone in town who might be familiar with this PI? A cop or someone?"

She braked at a stop sign and grinned at him. "You're brilliant."

Liam closed his eyes and leaned his head back. Not brilliant enough, he decided. Or he wouldn't be having all these doubts about who he was. While she drove, he forced his mind to go backward, to dig into his childhood. He focused on his dog, Sparky. He had loved that furry mutt. He relaxed and let the memories flow. For better or worse, he let himself float into the past.

THEN

Twenty-five years, one month ago...

ANDY SAT ON the porch. He felt sick. He wanted to cry but he was too big to cry. He dropped his head into his hands.

Sparky was gone.

He'd looked everywhere.

His dad had driven him all over the neighborhood. They had talked to all the neighbors and no one had seen him.

It was the worst day of his life.

"Come on, Andy, we've got stuff to do."

He raised his head and looked at Halle. He hadn't heard her walk up. "I don't feel like doing anything." He frowned at the big bag hanging around her neck. "What's that?"

"It's the stuff we gotta do." She sat down beside him and opened the bag. "I got Mom's little hammer. I got thumbtacks and I got tape. And these." She pulled out a paper and showed him.

He stared at the photo of Sparky and his stomach hurt. The flyer read, "LOST DOG. His name is Sparky. Please bring him home." Andy's name and address were under the photo. Then in big letters were the words "REWARD $20."

His eyes got big. "Is my dad offering a reward?"

"Uh-oh." Halle made a face. "I didn't think to ask him."

Andy's face puckered with disappointment. "Then what's this?" He pointed to the line about the reward.

"That's how much was in my piggy bank. Mom helped me count. Twenty dollars." She poked herself in the chest with her thumb. "I'm offering the reward."

Andy hugged her tight. "Thank you, Halle. You're the best friend ever."

She wiggled out of his arms. "Come on. We gotta put these up all over town. Mom's gonna take us."

Andy smiled. His eyes, burning again, forced him to blink them fast. "'Kay."

Hand in hand, they skipped over to her yard.

What would he do without Halle?

Chapter Eleven

NOW

Halle's detective friend was following up with a witness on another case but he promised to catch up with her as soon as he was finished. Until then, he suggested she wait at a place called the Pub on Eleventh Avenue South. It was close to his location.

Wasn't a hardship to hang out. The place was a British-style pub with a variety of cocktails, wines and whiskeys from which to choose. The atmosphere was not unlike one of the pubs he haunted back home. Lots of elegant wood details on the walls and around the bar. Upholstered chairs and classy tables. Soft music. People engrossed in conversation at the tables. The waiter had brought elegant stemmed glasses filled with sparkling water. Liam wasn't a big fan of the stuff, but it was something to do while they waited. Halle pretended to look over the menu, but she wasn't likely hungry any more than he was. They were basically killing time. Waiting to connect with yet someone else who might know some tidbit about Andy Clark's disappearance.

The lost boy.

Liam had almost ordered a whiskey neat but he'd talked himself out of it. He needed a clear head. But that trek down memory lane he'd taken while she drove across town had shaken him. The memory was vivid, too vivid. He'd been worried about Sparky and Halle had made posters offering a reward for the missing pup. There were parts of the memory that he could definitely say her words had prompted—had put the idea in his head—but there were others that had come straight from somewhere deep inside him. Straight out of his own past, or what felt like his past.

There had to be a way to unfurl these scattered clues and sensations and emotions so that he could look at them as a whole, rather than only in pieces. The fragments promised something they had not as of yet delivered—the whole story. As much as he wanted to dismiss his growing suspicions about his identity, there was something here. Some part of this was accurate and he needed to understand why.

Unless this PI or the detective had information that would point them in the right direction, he didn't see how he would ever know the whole story. There was, of course, the possibility that if any of this was actually true, his father may have confided in Penelope. But to interrogate her could cause her pain, he was sure. Why should he put her through that until he knew more?

Liam shook himself. What was he thinking?

His father would never have done this and if he was Andy, someone else had stolen him from the Clarks. But why wouldn't his father tell him if he was adopted or had been taken in under less than normal circumstances? Luke Hart had not been a liar or a kidnapper—he was a good man. A loving, compassionate man. That left no other option except his bio mom, but she had died when he was two.

Or had she?

He didn't remember her or her death. What if his father was covering for her?

Enough.

Liam pushed aside the troubling thoughts. He needed to focus on something else for a while. He leveled his attention on Halle and said, "Tell me about this Derrick Carson."

Halle looked up from the menu. "He's a detective with Metro."

Liam toyed with the stem of his glass. "I know that part. I mean, besides that. You laughed a couple of times when you were talking to him. Sighed one of those little breathy whispers. Fiddled with your hair. You two have a thing?"

"Breathy whispers?" She laughed, then clasped her hands atop the menu as if she worried she might reach up and fiddle with her hair again. She did that when she was thinking, he had noticed. What had she been thinking when the detective was chattering away in her ear?

She moistened her lips and looked directly at him. "No. We do not and never have had a *thing*. He has asked me out to lunch or dinner, to a movie once, but I've always declined. He's a friend. Nothing more."

"Ah." Liam nodded. "The detective has a thing for you but you don't feel the same way. Maybe he's still hoping you'll change your mind."

She smiled and shook her head. "The *detective* is a nice man who dates lots of women, but I never wanted to be one of his women."

"A player," Liam suggested.

"A player," she agreed. "But he's a good cop. We can trust him."

As hard as he tried to stay away from the subject of those unsettling memories that had haunted him today, Liam couldn't keep them out of his head. "When the dog went missing," he began, determined not to use the name Sparky, "you mentioned that was a few weeks or a month before Andy disappeared."

"Three weeks," she said. "Andy was devastated. I wanted to do something to help. My family and I had searched with him and his family but Sparky seemed to have vanished. So I took all the money out of my piggy bank and my mom helped me make flyers offering a reward for his return." Her face turned sad. "We really tried but we could never find him, and the next thing I knew, Andy was gone, too."

He nodded, his throat too tight, too dry to respond. His memory was accurate. Real. Too real.

She stared at him for so long he had to look away.

"Can you still pretend I'm wrong? That you aren't Andy?"

"Liam," he reminded her. "Liam Hart. I'm not Andy Clark." The words ripped from his aching throat, tasted bitter on his tongue.

"Is it because you don't want to think that the man you believed to be your father stole you from your real family?"

"That man was my real family." Liam spoke louder than he'd intended. A couple at another table glanced their way. "Sorry," he said to Halle. "I can show you photos of my father when he was a young man and a child. I looked just like him. Same hair, same eyes. Same dimple in the chin." He tapped his chin. "I don't know how to explain all these other flashes of—" he shrugged "—insight into the childhood you shared with Andy, but I am telling you my father was Luke Hart."

"Andy's dad, Andrew Clark, had blond hair and blue eyes, too. No dimple, not a chin one anyway. I've seen pictures of him as a young man and maybe one as a child. I can't say that he and Andy looked very much alike beyond their coloring. Andy's features were more like his mother's—like Nancy's. Her hair was darker than his when she was very young, her eyes a shade or so lighter. No dimple, either. The similarities were more in facial structure. The jawline, the nose."

"Well, there you go." He relaxed more fully into his chair. "My father and I could have been twins."

She sat quietly for a minute or so, watching him, assessing him.

"Go ahead." He sipped his water. "Say it."

"We have to do the DNA. It's the only way you'll ever know for sure."

He drew in a deep breath. "What about extended family? Did the Clarks have any siblings? Cousins? Any family that you're aware of."

"None. They were both only children and their parents had passed before Andy was born."

How convenient. His instincts stirred. He was onto something but he couldn't quite put his finger on what that something was. "They moved to Winchester from Nashville when Andy was eighteen or nineteen months old."

"Nineteen," Halle confirmed.

"Were they ever visited by out-of-town company? Maybe old friends from Nashville. Even if their parents had passed, surely they had friends. Colleagues? People from the church they attended?"

Her brow lined as she considered his question. "I can't remember anyone visiting them. Let me call Mom and ask."

She dug into her bag and withdrew her phone. Before she could call her mom, it vibrated in her hand and the screen lit up.

"Hello."

She listened for half a minute, then thanked the caller and disconnected. Her gaze locked with his. "That was Austen's neighbor. He's home."

Liam left a bill on the table for the water and a tip and they were out the door.

Halle drove slightly above the speed limit to arrive at the duplex in the shortest time possible but the driveway was empty. As she and Liam exited her car, the neighbor bounded out her front door, wiggling dogs in her arms.

"He didn't stay long," she explained. "He went in the house, came out with his suitcase and drove away. I tried to wave. Holler at him but he didn't even look back. I got a feeling whatever is on his tail, he don't want to be caught. Something ain't right. I've known him too long. This ain't like him."

Halle had a feeling the lady was more right than she realized. "Thank you. Please, call me if he or someone else shows up."

"I sure will," the lady promised.

Halle hesitated, turned back to her. "What kind of car does he drive?"

"A black four-door Ford Taurus. Had it forever."

"Thanks again!" Halle waved and hurried to the car and slid behind the wheel. Liam was already in the passenger seat. "Let's check his office again," she said as they snapped their seat belts into place. She tossed her bag onto the back floorboard and placed her cell on the console. "His neighbor is right.

Sounds like he's on the run. We should have staked him out instead of going after my detective friend," she said with regret.

"He could be headed to the airport for all we know."

She backed out of the driveway and pointed her car in the direction of Nolensville Pike. No way was she letting this guy get away.

"If he's headed to the airport, there's nothing we can do. Chances are we wouldn't catch him before he got through security. If we get to his office and he's not there—" she glanced at Liam "—I'm going in to see what I can find. If we're really lucky, he left something behind."

"I doubt your detective friend will be too happy about that move."

"Won't be an issue unless he finds out."

They exchanged a look. "In that case," he said with a widening grin, "I'm in."

Halle shook her head. It was very possible they would both be in jail before morning. As long as they had cells next to each other, she could live with that.

The traffic was heavier now. The quickest way across town to their destination was 440 but it would still take time. Halle merged into the traffic, her fingers tight on the steering wheel.

Her cell vibrated. She glanced at the screen. *Derrick*. She ignored it for now. There was no time to slow down. He would only want to know where she was. She would call him after...*this*.

By the time she reached the exit for Nolensville Pike her nerves were frayed. She had barely pulled onto the pike when traffic came to a dead stop. No! She clenched the steering wheel even tighter and leaned forward to see what was causing the bottleneck.

Blue lights…red lights throbbed in the distance. Police cruisers, two ambulances…a firetruck…this was bad.

"Looks like a major pileup," Liam said, taking the words right out of her mouth. "Hold on."

She turned to look at him as he was opening his door and standing up in the open doorway. She started to ask what the hell he was doing but before she could string the words together to rail at him he was getting back into the car.

"Three- or four-car accident. Injuries, from the looks of things. We're going to be here awhile."

Halle leaned her head back against the seat and groaned.

She had to do something. She checked her rearview mirror and then her side mirror. *Clear.* She eased into the right-turning lane and turned onto a side street that would take them away from this logjam.

No sooner than she turned, other cars started doing the same. The short street led around behind a gas station and intersected with Glenrose Avenue. She took a right on Glenrose and zigzagged over to Whitney Avenue. Whitney would take them beyond the accident and then they could take Vivelle back to Nolensville Pike.

Hopefully.

Her pulse was racing by the time she made all the turns and was back on Nolensville Pike heading toward their destination once more.

It would be dark in another hour and she had a feeling Frank Austen would be gone forever, taking whatever secrets he knew with him.

She slowed and made the turn into one of the few parking slots in front of the office. Austen's office was a part of one of those low, squat strip buildings from a long-ago era. There were bars on the plate glass windows as well as the doors. The sign was turned to the "Closed" side. There were only the five parking slots, not an actual parking lot, and all were empty except the one she'd used. On the opposite end was a vacant office. Across the street was a check-cashing place and a smoke shop.

They were out of the car and at the door and peering beyond the bars before either of them spoke. The deserted lobby was all that was visible from the front windows. A desk, a few chairs and a low table with a stack of magazines. From the dog-eared pages, she surmised they had likely been around a while. A single framed piece of artwork hung on the wall behind the desk. The decor looked as if it had been purchased at a budget motel fire sale.

"Come on," Liam said. "Let's see if there's parking or an entrance in the back."

Her heart thumping against her sternum, Halle followed Liam around the corner of the building.

A black Ford Taurus sat close to the building, the trunk lid raised. Halle's pulse jumped. He was here.

Liam was suddenly pulling her behind him. She wanted to ask why but decided if he had a reason, staying quiet was the better idea. They moved together, like the perfectly choreographed steps of a pair of cops entering a crime scene.

The back door was ajar. Halle knocked on it, causing it to push inward, and called out, "Mr. Austen! My name is Halle Lane. It's very important that I speak to you. We tried to call you!"

They waited. No answer. She called out again. Still nothing. Liam pushed the door fully open and eased inside. Halle stayed close behind him. The door led into a narrow corridor. The first door on the left was a bathroom. A few steps beyond on the right was a small lounge with a refrigerator and a microwave, a table and chairs.

The next door on the left led into a fairly large office. No windows. A long row of file cabinets stood against one wall. Shelves loaded with books and framed documents lined another. In the middle of the room was a long metal desk with two chairs flanking it and another behind it but pushed back so that it sat against a cluttered credenza.

Liam held up his hand. "Stay here."

She followed his gaze, noting the pile of folders on the desk that had been overturned.

He moved around the desk and grimaced. "You might want to call that detective friend of yours now."

Halle skirted the desk and considered the dead man on the floor. Definitely Austen. She had pulled up photos of him on the internet. He had one bullet hole in the center of his forehead. His unseeing eyes stared at the ceiling. His crumpled legs were tucked under him in an odd angle.

Liam knelt next to him and touched his carotid artery. "Definitely dead but he hasn't been for long. His skin is still warm."

A chill raced over Halle. The killer could still be nearby. She pulled out her phone and dialed Derrick's number. "Sorry I missed your call." The statement seemed ridiculous under the circumstances but she needed a moment to frame how to tell him about the dead man on the floor in front of her or how she'd entered the premises without an invitation.

"No problem. I'm at the Pub. I was just about to order another beer, where are you?"

"I'm at Frank Austen's office." She provided the address. "He's been murdered."

Derrick swore softly. "Don't touch anything. I'll call it in and head that way."

Halle put her phone away. "He said not to touch anything."

"We can look," Liam suggested, "as long as we don't touch, right?"

"I believe we can."

Austen had been going through his files. The pile that had fallen over had sent folders and their contents sliding over the floor. He had probably been looking for ones he wanted to take with him or destroy. No PI would want his work files discovered by just anyone who walked in, especially the police.

Halle read as many of the names on tabs as she could see. None were the Clarks. She moved to the file cabinets. She used the tail of her jacket to open first one drawer and then another. Liam glanced her way and she said, "I'm not touching it. My jacket is."

He laughed and started doing the same at the man's desk, except he used a tissue from the box on the credenza to keep his prints off the drawer handles.

When they had finished, they turned back to stare at the body on the floor. Liam said, "He could have something in his pocket. A thumb drive maybe."

Halle bit her lip. This would be their only chance to check. "That's possible."

The smell of gasoline and then a distinct whoosh resonated from the back of the building. They'd left the door open.

Halle started that way; Liam was close behind her.

The explosion that followed was loud enough to deafen anyone in or near the building. Liam yanked her back into the office. Debris showered down in the corridor. Liam's arms were around her, his body wrapped around hers like a shield.

For a few seconds she couldn't hear anything. Then there was the sound of flames hissing and sizzling. Liam stood, pulled her to her feet.

"Was that his car that exploded?" she asked.

"I can't imagine what else it would've been." He started forward again, moving toward the rear door through which they had entered. Halle stared at the pieces of metal and glass strewn across the floor. Damn. She'd been right. The killer had been hanging around.

Liam stayed in front of her. When they reached the door he looked out first. She poked her head between him and the doorframe. The Taurus was in flames. Sirens were shrieking in the distance.

"We should go around to the front," Halle said, surveying the area in hopes of spotting the culprit— possibly Austen's killer—responsible for that creepy feeling haunting her. Someone was watching them. She could still feel it. "Whoever did this might still be here."

When she would have stepped outside the door, Liam pulled her back. "Why don't we stay in here until the police arrive?"

Possibly he was right. Before she could say as much, a crash echoed from the lobby. Liam pushed her into the small lounge room.

Someone was still inside.

Breaking glass shattered the silence.

"Whoever it is, is trying to get out," Liam murmured.

Halle looked up at him. "If the police aren't out there by now, he'll get away."

"You're right." Liam opened the door. "I'm going after him."

Some deeply buried instinct surged and Halle grabbed him by the jacket. "Wait," she whispered.

He twisted to look at her. "Do you smell that?"

Was it the burning car?

Gasoline. Raw. Freshly spilled.

The whoosh that erupted next had Liam drawing back from the door he'd opened, ushering her back, as well. "We have to find a different way out of here."

Halle peeked past the still open door and quickly slammed it shut. Flames were rolling down the corridor, devouring anything in their path.

"We need to hurry!"

He rushed to the set of windows on the other side of the small lounge and unlocked first one and then the other. He pushed the sashes upward, the effort monumental since they clearly hadn't been opened in ages. There were no screens.

He turned back to her. "I'm going out first, just in case whoever did this is out there."

She started to argue but one long leg was already out the window. The other disappeared and he drew his upper body out. Halle glanced at the closed door, hoped no one burst through it or the flames crept under it. The smoke had already done so and invaded her lungs, making her cough.

"Come on!"

Liam reached through the window, grabbing for her.

She swung a leg over and through the opening. His hands were suddenly on her waist, lifting her away from the danger.

He pulled her away from the building until their bodies crashed into the end of the next one. The sun was setting, daylight going with it.

A shadow whizzed past the alley between the two buildings.

"Did you...?"

Halle didn't get to finish the question. Liam was already racing after the blur that had apparently been a person.

She rushed to the front corner of the building, glanced at her car, then in the direction Liam had gone.

She could follow in the car, catch up with him and whoever he was chasing.

Before the thought fully formed in her head, she was in the car and driving in the direction Liam had disappeared.

She caught sight of him.

There was another man. Dark tee. Dark jeans. Running like hell but Liam was gaining on him. Her heart started to pound. She floored the accelerator. The car lunged forward. When she was a good distance in front of the stranger, she whipped right and slammed to a stop on the sidewalk in front of him.

He almost ran into her car but he managed to skid to a near stop and slide past her front end.

Liam was hot on his trail.

She jumped out of the car and joined the chase. The man ducked into an alley. Liam followed. Halle pushed harder, plunged into the alley after them.

The blast of a gunshot had her hitting the ground.

Another shot. She gasped.

Liam!

She scrambled up and rushed forward. Liam had hit the ground, as well. Was he hurt? The other man had gone over the low wall at the end of the alley.

She couldn't chase him any longer. Had to make sure Liam was okay.

He was on his hands and knees now. Halle dropped to her knees beside him. "Are you hurt?"

He got to his feet. Offered his hand to her and pulled her up. "Just my pride. I almost had him when he drew his weapon and started firing. I had no choice but to hit the dirt."

Halle's knees tried to buckle.

Liam pulled her against him. "Steady there. You okay?"

She nodded, the move a little jerky. "Yes. I'm just glad you're not hurt."

The sound of sirens split the air and Halle felt ready to collapse. She leaned against Liam as they retraced their steps. She ignored her car, leaving it where it was for now.

For the first time since she started this investigation, she realized that there was at least one person who didn't want the truth to be found and was willing to take drastic steps to prevent that.

Mrs. Clark's murder could have been a robbery of some amount of cash she had hidden that no one had known about. Maybe a random act of violence.

But this, this was unmistakable.

This murder victim had something to hide.

Chapter Twelve

NOW

Derrick showed up while the firefighters were working to put out the fire. An ambulance had arrived.
Four police cruisers. Now the medical examiner's
van.

It was dark and the smells of burning wood, char-
ring metal and melting plastic were thick in the air.
The paramedics had insisted on checking Halle and
Liam for injury.

She wasn't injured. She was angry and frustrated.
Not to mention worried sick that yet another murder
had been committed because of her article.

What the hell was happening?

It was possible, she supposed, that none of this
was about Andy Clark or her investigation into what
happened to him…but every instinct she possessed
screamed differently.

This was about Andy. Her gaze landed on Liam

where he stood near one of the police cruisers, watching the activities going on around them. Someone did not want the truth to come out. Whatever secrets the past held, whatever evil had stolen Andy Clark, she had awakened that evil, and now two people were dead. If the man who died today, the PI Frank Austen, was the person who killed Mrs. Clark or been involved somehow, there remained at least one more someone who wanted to keep the past in the past.

The person who had either killed Austen or hired him killed.

Her gaze sought and found Liam once more. Her story, The Lost Boy, had set off a chain of events: Liam's appearance in Winchester, Mrs. Clark's murder and now the destruction of an office and the murder of the man who operated his business there. At this point, Liam surely understood that he was without doubt Andy Clark. The only person who could possibly want to keep that truth hidden was the person who took him as a child. His father was dead, so, obviously he wasn't the murderer.

But what about his stepmother? She was supposed to be in Paris. Was she capable of violence like this? Even simply hiring it done?

Would a person go that far—killing two people—to hide a twenty-five-year-old kidnapping? Would the statute of limitations have run out on the kidnapping? Why add two murders to the list?

There had to be more to the disappearance of Andy Clark than they knew.

"Let's go over this again, Halle," Derrick said. He settled on the dock bumper of the ambulance next to her.

"I've already told you everything," she reminded him. The truth was, she knew the routine. The police always repeated the same questions just to see if your answers were consistent. No matter that she and Derrick were friends, he had a job to do.

"You know the drill."

She did. She exhaled a weary breath. "As you know from the article I did on The Lost Boy, I'm digging around in the Andy Clark case."

He nodded. "What brought you to Nashville to talk to Austen?"

"My parents were friends, neighbors, with the Clarks. My mother remembered them going to a private detective when the police weren't able to find Andy. To follow up on that theory, I started with the one in Winchester my folks believed the Clarks had visited. He tried to help them but hit a brick wall, so he sent them to another PI in Tullahoma. The one in Tullahoma had recommended them to Austen."

"But you said he couldn't remember Austen's name."

There it was, an inconsistency. The man didn't miss a thing. Halle dipped her head. "Right. But he did remember the attorney who worked with the PI, David Burke."

Derrick shook his head. "Now that guy is a piece of work. I swear, I wouldn't put it past him to run for president in the next election. He's that cocky and has that kind of money."

"Yeah, I kind of got that impression," she agreed.

"You visited Burke and he gave you Austen's name."

"Yes, but the two haven't worked together in years. He said Austen had decided to go out on his own."

"When you were in Austen's office did you see anything I should know about that won't incriminate you or your *friend*?"

It would have been impossible to miss the emphasis he put on *friend* or the fact that he blatantly sent a look in Liam's direction. Men could certainly be territorial. Even when they didn't have the right.

"The front door was locked. The sign in the window was turned to Closed. But his neighbor had spotted him hauling a suitcase out of his house. She got the impression he was in a hurry, like someone was after him. Considering that information, we ignored the Closed sign."

Derrick quirked an eyebrow but said nothing.

"I suggested we go around back of his office to see if his car was here. It made sense that if he was making a run for it—for whatever reason—he might want to grab things from his office. You know, a file or part of some case that was important to him. Maybe a hidden stash of cash."

"Did you see a hidden stack of cash?"

"No." She smiled, indulging his teasing. "As I said, we came around to the back of the building and there was his car. I had asked the neighbor what kind of car he drove, so I recognized it immediately. The trunk was open, which suggested he was, indeed, in the office."

Derrick made that rolling motion with his hand for her to go on.

"We walked to the rear entrance. The door was ajar, so I knocked loudly and called out his name. I identified myself and said that I needed to speak with him. There was no response, so I waited a few seconds and called out again. It was clear something was wrong, so we went inside to check it out."

"It didn't occur to you to call the police and allow us to handle it? I was waiting for you at the Pub, you know."

Things could get sticky here. She shook her head. "Metro is busy enough without me calling to say a door is ajar on a business when the owner's car was clearly parked next to it. I figured he had his head in a filing cabinet or closet and just didn't hear me. How foolish would I have looked if I'd called it in and then your guys showed up and—"

"Okay, okay." He waved his hands back and forth. "I get it. But what I don't understand is why you didn't answer my call."

She frowned and decided on a fib. "You must

have called when I was out of the car speaking to the neighbor. I told you we went there first."

"Tell me again exactly what you saw inside and what happened from that point."

Halle went through the story again. From finding Austen's body, his car exploding and then the fire. The chase. She repeated all of it without missing an already stated detail.

Derrick made a few more notes and then heaved a sigh. "I guess that's it." He glanced at Liam, who hadn't moved. "You really think this guy is Andy Clark?"

She nodded. "I do. Back home, the chief of police is looking into it, as well." When he still looked skeptical, she went on. "You'd have to see the photos of him as a kid. It's him. I know it's him."

"Is he the reason no one else could hold on to you?"

Her gaze shot to the detective's. "What're you talking about? Remember, I was married."

"*Was* being the keyword." Derrick shook his head. "Really, this answers a lot of questions for me. I've heard you talk about this case dozens of times. But it wasn't until I saw you with him that I understood." He searched her face. "You've been in love with him since you were a kid."

"We were best friends, Derrick. Of course I loved him."

He smirked. "We are not talking about the same thing, Hal."

She pushed to her feet. "Can we go now? I have a long drive ahead of me."

He got up, put his hand on her arm. "Don't be angry with me. I'm just jealous."

She shook her head. "I'm not angry. Just exhausted and frustrated."

"Look." He glanced at Liam again. "Why don't the two of you stay at my place tonight? I'll see what I can dig up on Austen and we can catch up over dinner. How about it?"

"I really need any help you can give me about Austen." She braced for an argument. "But we should get going. The chief back home will be expecting to hear from me. My boss will want to know about my investigation so far. After all, this is work for me." The last part wasn't entirely true, but he didn't need to know that.

"All right. But next time I call, answer."

"I promise."

Before she could anticipate his move, he hugged her.

He drew back, held her arms. "Be careful and keep me up to speed on your investigation. We could work together and figure this out."

"Thanks, Derrick. I really appreciate it."

With a hasty goodbye she walked over to where Liam waited. "We can go."

"Good." He didn't look at her, just turned and started walking toward where they'd left her car angled across the sidewalk.

Halle followed.

She wasn't really surprised that he seemed more than happy to be getting out of here. She doubted this winemaker had ever chased after a bad guy or climbed out of a burning building. In her line of work she was accustomed to those sorts of intense scenes.

She could imagine him in the middle of a sprawling vineyard, working with the plants, testing the grapes. Peace and quiet. Beauty for as far as the eye could see.

This was a completely different world for him.

She'd taken his quiet, peaceful life and turned it into something painful and uncertain. He would probably hate her before this was over.

At the moment, she hated herself just a little bit.

HALLE'S ONLY REQUIREMENT for the hotel they selected was that they had room service and good beds. Fortunately, the hotel she'd always adored for their amazing beds and room service was available but there was only one room.

Great. Just great. As tired as she was, she stepped away from the counter to tell Liam. He'd gotten a call from his sister and had moved away from the registration desk for some privacy.

"Okay, sis. Don't worry." He smiled. "See you soon." He paused, listening. "Love you, too."

When he ended the call, Halle was smiling, too.

She couldn't help it. The sound of his voice, his smile, it made her feel safe and...

She cleared her head. "They have a room, but only one. There are two beds, however. Do you have a problem sharing a room?" She shrugged. "We could always drive home if you'd rather. Or find another hotel."

"No. This is fine. Driving back tonight would be pointless. We need to relax and talk. Anything but be stuck in a car for a couple of hours."

"And shower," she pointed out. Her gaze roved over him. They were both sweaty and smoky and...

She should get the room.

He passed her a credit card. "I don't want you paying for anything else."

She shook her head. "You flew all the way from California. Rented a car. I'd say you've paid more than your share already."

"Hal," he warned, "I'm paying."

She was too startled to argue with him further. Instead she took the credit card and walked back to the counter. This was the first time he'd called her Hal. He'd called her that all the time when they were kids.

Maybe he'd heard Derrick call her Hal.

No, she decided, it had come naturally because more memories were coming back whether he told her about them all or not.

When she'd taken care of the room, they headed

for the elevators. To her surprise the hotel boutique was still open.

"Wait. We need clothes."

She grabbed him by the arm and dragged him inside the chic shop.

"How may I help you?" The clerk grimaced before she could school the expression as she asked the question.

"I know," Halle said. "We were in a fire."

"Oh, my, I'm certainly glad you're all right."

"Thanks. We need a change of clothes. Underthings. Something to sleep in." She stared down at her feet. "Shoes if you have them."

The woman smiled widely and waved her arm. "I'm certain I have everything you need."

Halle wandered through the small women's section. She found jeans, a sweatshirt, ridiculously overpriced ankle boots. And, thank God, panties and one of those sports bras. She grabbed a nightshirt and she was good to go.

At the counter, the clerk was already ringing up similar items for Liam. Jeans, a sweatshirt, hiking shoes, tees and boxers. Socks. Oh, she forgot socks. She hurried back to the women's section and grabbed a pair. Back at the counter, the clerk reached for Halle's armload.

"I'll be paying for my own," she argued.

The clerk smiled again. "The gentleman insists on taking care of everything."

Halle glared at him. He grinned.

She was too tired to argue.

Finally, they were headed to the sixth floor. Halle leaned against the back wall of the elevator and closed her eyes. She tried to remember if she had ever been this tired. Maybe it was all the emotional turmoil making her so exhausted. She should call her mother in case their faces showed up on the news. Later, she decided, after a long, hot shower.

On the sixth floor, they walked silently to the proper door. Halle slid the key into the lock and waited for the green light. Inside, she tossed her bag onto one of the two beds. "You shower first," she said.

"I'm fine. You go first," he argued, dropping his bag onto the other bed.

"I'm serious," she said, "I'm going to take a while and I need to call home."

He held up his hands in surrender. "I'll go first." He grabbed his bag and disappeared into the bathroom. Seconds later she heard the spray of the shower.

The room was larger than the average hotel room. Another thing she liked about this hotel. She walked over to the floor-to-ceiling windows. She stared out over the sweeping views of the Cumberland River and the city's skyline. She had been so excited moving to Nashville after college and starting her first job as a reporter. She'd felt like her whole life was coming together in the picturesque city where anything could happen.

But at night, before she drifted off to sleep, she'd always thought of Andy. Wondered where he was and if he were safe and happy. In high school she'd made up stories about him. She alternated between him being in some foreign country as a spy or climbing mountains somewhere to break records. Sometimes, she decided he was a private investigator, helping lost children find their way back home because he never could.

She smiled, thought of all the ways she had imagined that they might meet again. In Paris at the Louvre. Or in Washington, DC, at the White House, or maybe in New York, atop the Empire State Building.

She'd kept a big notebook about him. Sometimes she would go months without writing in it, then she would think of him and write him a letter. It was silly and fantastical but she'd never been able to throw the letters away, or the notebook.

It was still at home, in the top of her childhood closet. She'd pulled it down for the first time in a while to start writing this anniversary story.

The pictures. She laughed. She'd put a picture in for each year he'd been gone. She'd also written about the big happenings in the world and the latest fashion and music trends as if he'd been kept in a cave or something.

She'd had no idea that he was just on the other side of the country, growing grapes.

The bathroom door opened and the fragrance of lavender soap and steam filled her senses. She turned around and watched as he scrubbed his damp hair with the towel. He wore one of the new cotton tees and boxers. His legs were as well muscled as his arms. She blinked the thought away, grabbed her bag from the bed and hurried across the room.

"My turn."

She hadn't even called her mom.

"Should I order room service?"

She paused at the door. "That would be great. Order me whatever looks good and lots of it."

He gave her a two-fingered salute and she backed into the bathroom, shut the door. She liked his hair when it was tousled like that. There were a lot of things she liked about him, like his hands and his eyes. Goodness, those eyes.

"Get ahold of yourself, girl."

While she sorted through her bag and removed tags from her purchases, she called her mom and let her know they were staying the night.

"Are you sure you're okay? You sound a little strange."

"I'm just tired." She broke down and told her about the private investigator and the fire. Her mother was, of course, horrified.

When she'd calmed her down over that event, her mom said, "I've been going through more of Nancy's papers. Chief Brannigan said I could go ahead. But I haven't found anything unusual or suspicious."

"Look for anything related to an attorney named Burke. David Burke."

"All right. Let me write down his name."

She waited for her mother to do so.

"Anything else, dear?"

She suddenly remembered Liam's question. "Did the Clarks ever have any old friends visit? Maybe from when they lived in Nashville. Could have been someone from the church they attended or business associates?"

"Funny that you asked. Your father and I talked about that from time to time. You know, before."

Before Andy went missing. All their lives were divided into two parts. Before and after he vanished.

"Did Dad remember anyone?" Halle felt herself holding her breath. The answer could be important. They might find someone else who knew the family from before they moved to Winchester.

"It was the strangest thing. They never had visitors. Not completely surprising since they had no relatives, just each other and Andy. But they were such social people. Always at church and attending community events. It seemed odd that they had no friends from Nashville who ever visited. Your dad said maybe something happened up there and they cut ties with friends and associates. It happens. Feelings get hurt, people refuse to get past the event."

Something like suddenly having a child without ever having been pregnant.

Halle caught her breath at the thought. "Thanks, Mom. You've been very helpful."

"Will you be home tomorrow?"

"I think so. Unless the police need us to stay for some reason related to the fire." She didn't mention the explosion. A fire was sufficient worry fodder.

"Drive safely and give Liam our love."

"I will. Love you."

Halle placed her phone on the marble counter. No matter how this turned out, Liam would be going back to his home. They were going to miss him desperately. Her heart heavy, she peeled off the smoky clothes and turned on the water.

The shower was like heaven on earth. Her body had needed the hot water so badly. Her muscles relaxed and she took her time, smoothing the soap over her skin and then shampooing her hair. She was grateful for the toiletry pack that included not only soap, shampoo and the usual, but disposable razors, as well.

By the time she was finished, her bones felt like rubber. She dried herself, slipped on underwear and the nightshirt and then used the hotel dryer to dry her hair. That part took the longest of all. When she exited the steamy bathroom the delicious aromas of room service had her stomach rumbling.

"Oh my God, that smells good." She rushed to the table where the silver service sat. "Why aren't you eating?"

"I was waiting for you." He joined her at the table. Ever the gentleman.

Halle curled her feet under her in her chair while Liam removed the covers from the dishes. Fish, chicken, vegetables. He had ordered all sorts of dishes and they all looked amazing.

"I thought we'd try a little of everything."

A bottle of white wine as well as a bottle of rosé had her licking her lips.

"I wasn't sure which one you preferred." He gestured to the iced-down bottles. "And I didn't forget dessert." The final lid revealed a heavenly-looking chocolate cake with fudge icing.

"I may die right now." She wanted to taste it all.

"Eat first." He placed a linen napkin over his lap and stuck his fork into a tiny, perfectly roasted potato. She watched him eat and it was the sexiest thing she had ever seen. She didn't fight it. Surrendered to instinct and that was how they ate. No plates, just taking whatever they wanted with a fork or fingers and devouring. They drank the wine and laughed at stories from their respective childhoods. From all the stories he'd told her, she could not wait to meet his sister, Claire.

By the time they were finished, she was feeling a little tipsy. The food was mostly gone and both bottles were drained. She felt more relaxed than she had in decades. They had discussed the day's events and Burke and Austen—and Derrick. The man was still convinced she had a thing for Derrick. No way. She'd also told him what her mom had to say about any friends from Nashville the Clarks might have had, which was none who ever appeared at their door. She and Liam agreed that was somewhat unusual considering how social the Clarks had been in Winchester.

"You know," she said, after polishing off the last of the wine in her glass, "I wrote you dozens of letters."

"Me?"

She frowned and shook her head. "Andy." Then she stared at him. "No. *You*. I mean you. Whatever you believe, I know you're him."

"Okay." He laughed, his eyes glittering with the soft sound.

God, his mouth was sexy when he was relaxed. She put her hand to her mouth just to make sure she hadn't said the words out loud.

"Tell me about the letters," he prompted.

"I told you what was going on in Winchester. Who was doing what at school. I even put pictures with the letters." She laughed. Placed her glass on the table. "It was silly, I know. But I wanted to still feel you and that was the only way I could."

She blinked. He had moved. He was suddenly next to her, on his knees, staring into her eyes, and her breath caught.

"I don't know if I'm this Andy you loved so much when you were a kid," he said softly, so softly she shivered, "but I would really like to be the guy you care about now."

Her heart swelled into her throat. She started to suggest that it was the wine talking, but it wasn't. The truth was in his eyes. Those blue eyes she knew as well as her own. And despite her wine consumption, she was stone-cold sober as she considered what could happen between them tonight.

"I'm really glad, because I would hate to think I'm in this alone," she confessed.

He kissed her so sweetly that tears stung her eyes. Then he stood and pulled her into his arms. He carried her to the nearest bed.

No matter what happened tomorrow, she would always cherish this night.

Chapter Thirteen

NOW

Napa, California

Claire Hart had not stopped pacing the floor since she spoke with Liam. From the moment he'd told her he was staying a few more days in Winchester she had gone through every possible hiding place in the house. There were no photos of Liam from the time he was a little baby—and there were only a few of those—to when he was around seven. There were some listed as being of him during that time period but never showing his face pointed at the camera.

She knew deep in her heart that something was wrong with this scenario.

Alone in this big old house, Claire had allowed her imagination to run away with her. She had searched everywhere, even in her parents' private space. She'd felt so guilty. How could she doubt her parents this way? What had possessed her to believe they would do such a thing—whatever the *thing* was? At the beginning, she had refused to label the notion driving her. But then she had been forced to concede that something was not as it should be. There were secrets.

Then she'd found that box.

Not a large box. More like one of the candy boxes with the double layers of candies and the map that told you what kind was in each slot of chocolate-covered goodies.

She stared at the offending box now. After picking through it, falling apart a little more with each new discovery, she had pulled herself together and brought it to the family room. She had placed it on the coffee table while she decided what to do about it. She stared at it now with its faded gold coloring and painted red ribbon. This box was evidence of the most shocking secret she could possibly have imagined.

Several scenarios had gone through her head when she'd been poking around, but nothing like this. She shuddered. This just couldn't be.

She needed to call Liam.

No, no, she couldn't call him. This wasn't something she could tell him over the phone. She had to go to Winchester and *show* him. He needed to see this with his own eyes. She would not be the one to say out loud the words that were his real story.

She couldn't. She loved her brother far too much.

Stop, just stop. If she didn't stop this confounded pacing she was going to wear a path in her mother's favorite Persian rug. She twisted and started back the other way. Not possible. She had to keep moving to prevent exploding.

It might not be a bad idea to call Halle Lane. The way Liam had spoken about her when he'd called earlier, it was obvious he thought she hung the moon. Claire could put this monkey on her back. She was the one who'd started this after all, with her search for the truth.

Claire's stomach twisted with a thousand tiny knots. The truth was painful and startling and their lives would forever be changed when it was revealed, and she saw no way around it coming out.

She paused to stare at the box. She could not pretend she hadn't found it.

The sound of the front door being unlocked snapped her from the troubling thoughts. Fear seared through her veins. Why hadn't she set the security system? She had locked the door, hadn't she?

Claire grabbed her cell, ready to dial 911 as she eased to the entry hall.

The door opened.

She stalled, unable to move.

Her mother. What was she doing home?

Outrage blasted her before she could temper it. "What're you doing back? I thought you were headed to London next."

She reminded herself that this was her mother

and that she loved her. She had always been a good mother to both Claire and Liam.

But she had lied. Fury flashed anew inside Claire. Her mother had hidden the truth all these years.

Penelope gave her a quick smile. "I'll explain later. I'm in a bit of a hurry right now."

She rushed past. Claire frowned. Where were her bags? Still in the car? Wouldn't the driver have brought them in? She walked to the door and peered out the side glass. Taillights faded in the distance.

What on earth?

She pivoted and stormed after her mother. She wasn't in the family room or the kitchen. "Mom?"

No answer. Claire headed toward her bedroom and found her standing on a chair, poking around in the top of her closet.

"Looking for something?" Claire asked, unable to conceal the suspicion in her tone.

"Yes...there's a box." Penelope kept pawing through hat boxes and handbags, her movements frantic.

"It's in the family room," Claire announced. She might as well put her mother out of her misery.

Penelope stilled, turned to stare down at her.

"I'll be waiting there." Claire turned away from her. She strode out of the room, a volatile mixture of emotions fueling her. Anger and disappointment and something like disgust.

A minute or so passed before her mother joined her. Claire didn't have to be in the room to know she would have put the chair back where it belonged, shut off the closet light and closed the door. Her mother was particular like that.

When Penelope paused at the sofa, her gaze fell upon the box.

The box.

The nine-by-fifteen-inch cardboard container that held the incredible lie that was their life.

"Apparently you opened it," she said, her voice brittle, too faint.

Penelope Hart stood there with her matching silk trousers and blouse and perfectly made-up face and hair. She was beautiful. Elegant. Loving. Patient. Kind. Supersmart.

And a liar.

"What does this mean?" Claire demanded.

Her mother's gaze lifted from the box to meet Claire's. "I will tell you everything on the way to the airport."

Did she really believe she could just leave right now? Good God, it was almost ten o'clock. "You are not leaving until you explain this—" she gestured to the damned box "—to me."

"I have to get to Winchester. There's a flight just after midnight that would put me in Nashville around nine in the morning. I cannot miss it. I have to speak to Liam." She shook her head, the move so faint Claire might not have noticed had she not been glaring at her mother. "Please tell me you haven't told him about this."

How dare she make such a plea!

"I haven't told him," Claire snapped. "I didn't want to be the one to shatter him." Tears burned in her eyes. "Tell me how this is possible!"

Her mother walked to her then, grasped Claire's arms in her hands and held her tight. "I need you to trust and believe in me—"

"Are you kidding?" The tears streaked down Claire's face. She could not hold them back. "How will I ever trust you again?"

A single tear slid down her mother's cheek. "I promise I will explain everything. Please, just come with me and I'll tell you on the way to the airport."

Claire pulled free of her grasp and snatched up the box. "You can tell me on the way to the airport, but I'm going with you to Winchester."

"Claire—"

"Someone needs to be there for him," she argued. "Someone who hasn't lied to him."

Chapter Fourteen

NOW

Sunday, March 15
Winchester, Tennessee

Halle had never been so glad to be home.

She turned all the way around in her apartment above the garage. All these months she had felt as if she'd failed in her career and that being back here was evidence of that failure. A smile spread across her lips. But it wasn't a failure. It was meant to be. Liam was going to stay with her a few more days until they sorted things out. Later today he had to call his sister and his stepmom to talk and then…

Well, she didn't know where they went from there, but whatever happened, it would be good. Wonderful. And full of possibility.

A soft sigh seeped out of her. She had never been happier. She was still a little afraid of how things would turn out. There remained a lot of questions. Liam wanted to do the DNA test before confronting his stepmother with any hard questions. Which was totally understandable. There were still so many unknowns…the perpetrator in Mrs. Clark's murder, for one.

Despite the heinousness of the poor woman's murder as well as Austen's, Halle experienced a strange serenity she'd rarely felt before.

Since waking up this morning she had walked around with a goofy grin on her face, but she wasn't the only one. Liam wore the same happy face. They'd had breakfast in the room and then dressed and driven back to Winchester. Bursts of animated conversation had been followed by lapses into satisfied silence.

Her biggest regret was that they had missed all those years between when he vanished and now. She walked over to her desk to start going through her notes. Laundry could wait. She wanted to get as many of her thoughts down as possible while it was all still fresh.

Liam had just left to get his things from the hotel and to check out. A local agency had agreed to take care of his rental car. Her parents had already left for church by the time they arrived back in Winchester this morning. She couldn't wait to tell them that she and Liam were going to start seeing each other seriously.

The whole idea was a little unsettling when she

considered that he lived in California and she lived here…but they would work it out. Somehow.

Everything felt right.

A knock on her door startled her. She pressed her hand to her chest and reached for calm. She'd been jumpy this way since Liam left. She had to get a grip. He was just going across town. He would be back soon. Probably within the hour.

She pushed away from her desk and went to the door. Maybe her parents were home from church already. She opened the door wearing that big old smile, ready to tell her mom—

It wasn't her mom.

"Mr. Burke." She frowned. Surprised—no, shocked—to find the big-shot attorney standing on her landing.

"Ms. Lane, I'm so glad I was able to catch you."

Halle composed herself once more. This was odd. Something wasn't right. "What is it?" If he'd come all this way, surely he had an update for her that might prove relevant to their ongoing search. "Tell me."

He hesitated, made a face. "My time is really short, Ms. Lane, but it was vitally important that I speak to you in person. This is not the sort of thing to be done by phone."

"Okay." Her instincts stirred. Some part of this picture wasn't quite right.

"Can you take a ride with me? There's something you need to see."

Now she was straight up worried. "What's going on?"

"Please." He stepped back from the door and gestured to the stairs. "Let me show you. There's really no way to explain this without showing you."

Every instinct she possessed warned that she should be suspicious—maybe even afraid—but this was the one man who might be able to shed light on what really happened twenty-five years ago.

"Just tell me. That will be faster." If his time was so short, then talking to her right here was the quickest way to give her whatever information he was so eager to share.

She wasn't about to go anywhere with him. Particularly since his former investigator had been murdered not so long after she visited this man.

He pulled a gun from his pocket and pointed it at her. "We do this my way. Get your keys. We'll take your car."

Moving slowly, deliberately, as she tried to think of what to do, she crossed the room and grabbed her shoulder bag, tucking her cell into it.

"All right," she said, turning back to him.

"Ladies first," he told her, waving the gun toward the stairs.

They descended the stairs and strode across her backyard. "Where are we going?" The more she knew, the better. Maybe she could stop this before they got too far. Now she was glad her parents were out. She wouldn't want them in danger.

"It's not far," Burke said rather than answer her question.

Once they were in the car, she pulled out her cell. "I should let Liam know. He'll wonder why I'm not home."

"Drive," he suggested. "You'll want to hear me out first. There are things you need to think long and hard about before you speak with him."

What did that mean? She tamped down her fears and focused on getting away, putting distance between herself and her parents' home before they arrived.

She reached way down deep for calm. Struggled to keep her voice steady. "Why don't you tell me what's going on? And why you felt the need to use force to have me go with you?"

He buckled himself into the passenger seat, keeping the gun trained on her. "No questions now. Just drive."

She backed out of the driveway and then remembered to fasten her seat belt. Not easy with one hand.

"Which way are we headed?"

"Keep going the way you are, then turn right at the intersection."

She did as he asked. When he still offered no explanation for where they were going, she said, "You came a long way. I'm assuming this is important. Maybe about your PI friend who was murdered?" She wanted to learn as much as she could, even as her mind raced, trying to figure out what to do.

He nodded, his expression somber. "It's a real shame."

"The two of you worked together for a long time—before he went out on his own, I mean."

"Decades. He was the best investigator I ever employed. Make a left at the light." He shook his head. "But he got sloppy toward the end. I had ignored a mistake here and there over the years, but it became too much."

Halle glanced at him. "That's too bad."

"You can only overlook so much before you realize that the situation is becoming a serious liability."

She nodded as understanding dawned. He'd killed Austen. She needed to stop Burke before he killed her too.

"Turn left here onto 16."

She tensed. Keith Springs Road, Highway 16, would take them out of town. "Where are we going?"

"I had to drive down very early this morning," he said rather than answer her question about where they were going. "I had to find the right spot." He glanced at her. "That was particularly important." Then he surveyed the interior of the car. "Choosing a means of transportation that wouldn't be connected to me was important, too. I learned a few things from Austen over the years. There are all sorts of people you can hire to do these sorts of things. But some aspects I prefer to handle personally. It's better that way. No worries of anyone talking. No potential witness."

Fear bolted through her. She slowed for the turn. Her heart thumped so hard she could hardly breathe.

He pressed the muzzle of the handgun to her temple. "Do exactly as I say. Do not doubt as to whether I'll use this or not."

Halle stared straight ahead and started moving forward again. "Whatever you say," she said tightly. "But I need you to lower the weapon."

He pulled the gun away from her head but kept it in his hand, laying on the console between them. "Then drive until I tell you otherwise. Drive carefully and within the speed limit."

She did as he asked, potential scenarios for escaping swirling through her head.

"When I first started out, I was a little fish swimming in a big pond," he began as she drove farther along a road that went up the mountain and eventually across the wildlife refuge into Alabama. Once they were beyond the Keith Springs area there was basically nothing but woods and the occasional trail hunters used.

She had to find a way to get away from him…to warn Liam. But she couldn't get the gun away from him here. He'd overpower her quickly. He had an iron grip on his weapon.

"But I was determined to make myself indispensable," he went on. "All I had to do was find the right niche. After a few not-so-successful starts, I found the perfect one. All those rich people in Nashville. There had to be a way to tap into those resources in a way that cut right to the heart. You know, people are far more generous when emotions are involved." He laughed. "Luckily for me, there were plenty among them who suffered from one fertility issue or another. Not to mention the ones who just didn't want to put their bodies through the trauma of carrying a child and then giving birth. There are those unsightly stretch marks and such."

Halle set her fear aside and glanced at him. Playing to his ego would work to her benefit. "You became the go-to attorney for private adoptions."

"Oh, did I. I took every opportunity to offer what no one else could or would. You know, it's amazing what people will gladly pay to get exactly what they want. The problem to overcome was availability. There's not always a child with precisely the desired features. Just the right color hair or eyes isn't such a huge obstacle, but a clean bill of health from the bio parents. Maybe taller parents or certain dimples or—" he glanced at her "—freckles. Sometimes they were just looking to replace the child they'd lost with one that resembled him or her as closely as possible."

The reality of what he was saying filtered through the desperation pounding at her skull. "You had to find the perfect child."

"To the letter. The more specific the request, the more expensive the product."

Product? They were talking about children here. Her stomach turned in disgust. "Not such an easy order to fulfill."

"Tell me about it. There are some self-centered people in this world. You combine that sort of selfishness with money and you have customers desperate to throw that money around. But Frank, he was good. He had the process down to a science. I gave him very specific parameters from the beginning. The children could only be taken from people who were dirt-poor or homeless or just plain bad. The kind with no means to pursue a real search and the type the police wouldn't likely believe. People who shouldn't have had kids in the first place. The only time he was allowed to go outside those parameters was if the requested product could not be found otherwise. Frank would go all over the place. He never shopped in the same town twice or in places too close together. He was very careful. At least, most of the time."

Halle felt sick. The mere idea of all the people whose children had been snatched from them made her soul ache. What kind of monsters did this sort of thing and dared to look at it as simply supply and demand?

Whatever it took, she was going to take this scumbag down.

"I appreciate you sharing your career-building experience," she said, summoning her bravado and going for nonchalance, "but what does this have to do with me? I didn't even get a chance to talk to Mr. Austen. He was dead when we arrived."

Burke glanced at her then. "Take the next right."

Heart in her throat, she slowed and made a right turn onto a narrow dirt road. She drove slowly until she reached a gate.

"Stop right here."

She did as he asked, put the car into Park and shut off the engine. *Think, Halle!* There was the gun. He had the upper hand, for sure. But she was younger and more physically fit. She could outrun him if she got a chance.

Liam was waiting for her. She would not let him down. She would make the opportunity to escape. They were not losing each other again.

Burke nudged her with the barrel of the weapon. "Don't forget I have this. If Frank were here, he could tell you I know how to use it."

She nodded and he motioned with the weapon. "Get out and bring your cell phone with you."

He kept the weapon trained on her as she got out. He did the same, scrambling across the console and out of the car on her side, not once allowing his aim to deviate from her.

"Now, this is what's going to happen, Ms. Lane. You're going to call your friend from Cali and tell him to meet you here. That your car has broken down. Once he arrives—"

"No." She shook her head. "I won't do it." She might not be able to escape this bastard but she was not bringing Liam into it. She had already turned his life upside down; she would not summon him into a trap.

"Do it." He pressed the muzzle to her forehead. "Now."

"Okay." She took a deep breath. "I will on one condition."

"Not that you're in any position to be tossing out conditions, but let's hear it."

"Tell me how Frank got Andy."

He laughed. "Oh, that was his first mistake. Under no circumstances was he to ever kill anyone to obtain the product."

She shook her head. "There must be some mistake. No one was killed when Andy was taken."

"You see," Burke countered, "that's because he wasn't Andy the first time he was taken."

LIAM WAS SURPRISED to find Halle's car gone when he returned to her apartment. He paid the fare and thanked the driver. The Lanes weren't back from church, either. He glanced around the yard. Maybe she'd run to the store for a few items. She'd mentioned being out of everything.

As he climbed the stairs that same grin that had been tugging at his lips all morning appeared again. It was a little crazy, he was aware. He'd met Halle only three days ago and he felt things for her he had never felt for anyone. But he had known her before. Somehow, however, he wanted to deny the possibility that he was this Andy Clark. As he lay in bed last night with her in his arms so many memories had flooded him. There was no denying that truth.

There was only the question of how it had happened.

When he reached the door, he hesitated. She hadn't given him a key. There hadn't been any need.

What if something had happened to her parents?

Worry gnawed at him. A car accident or something? But why wouldn't she have called him?

He tested the doorknob. To his surprise it was unlocked. He went inside and all looked as it had when he left. He walked around the apartment, didn't spot a note. Okay, so she had likely just run to the store for milk or something.

Maybe he'd call her.

The sound of a car door slamming had him heading back to the door. He was halfway down the steps before he realized the car in the driveway wasn't Halle's. The woman striding toward him wasn't Halle, either… It was Penelope. Moving up beside her was Claire.

What the hell?

"Liam!" Claire shouted as she broke into a run.

He met her at the bottom of the steps. She hugged him hard. He hugged her back, his eyes still on his stepmom. "Hey, sis. What're you guys doing here?"

Had they decided he'd lost his mind and planned an intervention? Surely Penelope wouldn't have returned from Paris just because Liam had taken some time off to pursue a mystery that she couldn't possibly know the full ramifications of…

Unless his sister had called her.

As if she'd sensed his realization, Claire drew back, looked him square in the eyes. "We need to talk."

Penelope hugged him next, smiling warmly. "It's good to see you."

What was going on here?

"Come on in." He gestured for the two to go up the stairs before him. He'd left the door standing wide open in his haste to get outside and meet Halle.

She would be back any minute, he was certain. Turned out, he realized as he walked into the apartment to join Claire and Penelope, that it was probably a good thing Halle wasn't home at the moment. These two had something on their minds and he had a feeling it wasn't going to be good.

"What's going on?" He closed the door and moved toward the sofa. "Sit. You must be tired after that flight. What'd you do, take a red-eye?"

"Where's the reporter?" Claire glanced around the apartment.

"Halle will be back in a few minutes."

Penelope had already perched on the edge of the sofa. When Claire did the same, Liam sat down facing them. Claire removed her backpack and started to open it.

"Seriously," he said when neither of them spoke, "what's going on?"

Claire pulled out an old candy box. The gold-colored kind with the painted red ribbon. Looked vintage.

Penelope placed her right hand on the box, seemingly stopping Claire from whatever she'd intended next. "Claire told me about the article, Liam, and why you've come to Winchester."

He nodded, but before he could comment, she went on, "There are things I should have told you right after your father died." She exhaled a big breath. "I always felt he should tell you but he didn't want to unsettle your life, so he kept his secret and I stood by his decision."

Claire glared at her. "Just tell him already."

Worry and fear and a number of other emotions he didn't fully comprehend twisted inside him. "What're you trying to tell me?"

"Not long after you were born, Luke and your birth mother, Tara, found themselves in a very bad place financially. They were homeless and living in the woods, camping, surviving on next to nothing. Luke was looking for work. After the vineyard where he'd worked since he was a child was sold, he was let go, no matter that he was the manager. The news was shocking and, worse, he wasn't able to find work. It was a difficult time for everyone in the business, but especially for your parents since they had a baby."

Liam felt as if he were outside his body watching this scene. He wanted to ask questions but he couldn't form the words. Claire stared at him as if he'd just been told he had terminal cancer.

"Tara was having real problems," Penelope said.

"She was sick much of the time and your father was very worried. So much so that he broke down and called his sister—"

"Sister?" Claire demanded before Liam managed to find his voice again. "You didn't tell me that part. You were supposed to tell me everything on the plane."

Penelope ignored her and went on. "Your father had a sister but they had been estranged for years. I don't know the reason. He would never speak of it. But because he was so worried about your mother and, obviously, you, he made the call. He asked for her help but she refused."

The hurt his father must have felt was like a sucker punch to his gut. He could only imagine his level of desperation, and Liam feared he already knew where this was going.

"Your father soldiered on, finding odd jobs to feed his family. But one day, when you were only fifteen months old, he came home and the two of you were missing."

"Missing—" Liam suddenly found his voice "—as in my mother ran away and took me with her or missing like someone took us?"

"Your father had no idea. He was terrified that because she had been so sick, primarily with very serious postpartum depression, she had decided to leave. Perhaps go home to her mother who was still alive at the time. But she wasn't at her mother's. He searched and searched and searched. The police helped for a while as did some of his old friends from the vineyard where he'd worked so many years, but the two of you were not found. He never stopped looking, but eventually he had to move on or lose his mind."

She paused for a moment and Liam felt certain he should say something, but he had no idea what to say. A million little things were going through his head but none of them seemed exactly right. He should call Halle. Find out why she wasn't here yet. She would be able to put all this into perspective. His emotions kept him from finding his footing. Judging by Claire's expression, he felt she was in the same boat with him.

"After two years of watching things fall apart, the new owner of the vineyard had decided he wasn't cut out for the business, so he sought out the former manager, your father, and made him an offer he couldn't refuse. Just to get the place off his hands, he would sell him everything—at a steal of a price—if he would promise to make up the difference when and if he ever got things running in the black again. Luke accepted his offer and threw himself into his work. It was the only way he maintained his sanity. We met shortly after he started. It was a couple of years before he shared the agony of losing you and his wife. The vineyard was back in the black and things were going extremely well. I suppose this allowed him to look back at his painful loss. I desperately wanted to help and I had a few contacts from my time in LA. I had worked in an attorney's office and he had had the very best investigators. I asked him to help us find the truth."

Liam braced himself. For days now, he had wanted to know the whole truth. Suddenly he wasn't so sure.

"Another year was required for the investigator to find someone who had seen something the day you and Tara disappeared, but he did. Even more time was required to track down who that person the witness had seen was. This unknown person turned out to be a PI from Nashville, a Frank Austen."

Liam's heart dropped into his stomach. "Austen is dead."

Penelope made a face but then kept going. "On your father's behalf, my friend made a deal with Austen—he wouldn't go to the police as long as Austen told him what happened to you." Penelope took a moment before going on. "You were the target of one of Austen's searches for a child that was wanted by a couple unable to have their own. Austen waited for an opportunity when Luke was not around and he attempted to take you. But your mother was tougher than she looked. She fought him. He swore it was an accident, but, sadly, he killed her. Took her body with him and buried her. Then he took you to his boss, who presented you to his clients, Nancy and Andrew Clark."

Liam closed his eyes. His mother was dead, his father had suffered unspeakable pain because the

Clarks wanted a child. He was going to find David Burke and beat the hell out of him. "Why didn't my father see that Austen went to jail for what he'd done? That PI friend of yours had no business making that deal."

"Liam, he did what he had to do to find you. Nothing else mattered to your father at that point. Not revenge, not even justice. Only finding you."

"So the Clarks were destroyed because no one wanted to go to the police and do this right? My God, they wouldn't have wanted to adopt a child who had been taken under those kinds of circumstances. What you did only hurt another family."

And stole his life.

Penelope drew back at his heated words. "Your sympathies are misplaced, Liam."

Liam felt sick. This was wrong. All of it. He wouldn't have believed his father capable of this sort of underhandedness, no matter the motive. Why hadn't he gone to the Clarks and told them the truth? They could all have worked together to resolve the situation. He glared at his stepmother. "What does that even mean?"

"Nancy Clark was your father's sister. She had, it seemed, been trying to have a baby for years and couldn't. When she found out Luke had a child and was in trouble financially, she decided he didn't deserve the child. She and her husband hired David Burke and his investigator to find you and take you."

Another of those sucker punches landed to his gut.

"When your father found out, he started planning how to get you back. Though he hated his sister for what she had done, she was still his sister and he didn't want her to end up in prison. He took you back. I helped him. And then he called Nancy and told her that if she ever came near you again, he would go to the police with all the evidence he had. She agreed, but she asked for only one thing, that she receive an occasional photo so she could see you grow up, so to speak, and know you were all right." She gestured to the candy box Claire held. "All the evidence, the signed agreement they reached, photos, articles, a journal from your mother, is there when you're ready to look at it."

Liam pushed to his feet, couldn't remain seated a moment longer. "I have to call Halle."

"I am so very sorry, Liam," Penelope said. "He never wanted you to know. The both of you had suffered enough. It was difficult at first, yes. But he was always gentle with you, and slowly but surely you forgot about that other life and came back to him. His son. The one stolen from him. There was only ever one frightening incident. You tried to run away and were hit by a car. You had no life-threatening injuries but you had a concussion and a broken arm. Oddly enough, after that you were fine. It was as if you locked away the life with the Clarks and became Liam again."

He wasn't sure he would ever understand how his mind had hidden so much from him. His cell vibrated with an incoming text and he pushed the disturbing thought away. *Halle*. He frowned as he read her message.

Car won't start. Can you come pick me up? Take Highway 16. Go eight miles and take dirt side road on right just past mile marker sign. I feel like an idiot.

His frown deepened. "I have to pick up Halle. I need to borrow your rental. As soon as we get back, we'll figure this out."

"I'm going with you." Claire set the candy box aside and grabbed her backpack.

Liam shook his head. "I need to tell her myself. We'll all talk when we're back."

Claire handed him the keys to the rental outside. "We'll be waiting."

He accepted the keys. "Thanks."

At the door, Penelope's voice stopped him, "Whatever you're feeling right now, please keep in mind that your father and your bio mom loved you more than you can possibly imagine. Even Nancy loved you. She was just a selfish woman who wanted to hurt her brother."

Liam nodded. "I know they loved me." His gaze held hers for a moment longer. "I know you do, too. That means a great deal to me even if I'm not doing a very good job of showing it right now."

Penelope nodded. Her lips trembled as she smiled. "Be careful."

"I'll be back in a few minutes." He winked at Claire. "Love you, too."

Chapter Fifteen

NOW

Halle couldn't be sure how much time had elapsed, but she was certain it was enough for Liam to be close even if he made a wrong turn or two before finding the correct dirt road. This road wasn't very long. Maybe a quarter of a mile before the locked gate prevented going any farther. Burke had marched her far enough into the woods that they wouldn't be spotted immediately when Liam arrived, but they could see her car from where they waited. The woods around them, however, were so dense it would be impossible to see her car from the main road. No one passing by would spot them.

When she had refused to call him, Burke had sent a text. Bastard.

He had made two calls on her cell after that. He'd spoken to someone on one of the calls but not on the other one. Since everyone was aware that cell calls could be traced back to a location, she suspected he was attempting to lay the groundwork for either his alibi or for framing someone else.

What a low-down scumbag.

"I don't get it," she said, breaking the extended silence. She needed him focused on something else rather than watching her. Time was running out. Desperate measures were her only recourse. In order to avoid ending up dead before she drew him away from this location, she had to distract him.

"You don't get what?" he demanded. "Not that it matters." The way he looked at her as he said this was warning enough that he didn't expect her to leave this mountain outside a body bag.

"Why go to all this trouble? Frank Austen is the one who murdered the kid's mother. Not you. Besides, that was a really long time ago. Even if someone remembered he worked for you back then, it likely wouldn't matter."

He laughed. "If only it were that simple." He pointed at her with the gun. "This is your fault, anyway. If you hadn't written that article, maybe none of this would have happened."

She shrugged, pretending she didn't get it. "What does my article have to do with any of this?"

"It was all over the place," he snapped. "Austen got nervous. He had a feeling the old lady was up to something. So he paid her a little visit to remind her about their deal and then he saw the kid all grown up visiting you. He understood then and there what she'd done. He called me whining like a little baby and I told him to clean it up. It was his mess, not mine."

"He killed her." Halle had never wanted to hurt anyone the way she did this man.

"I couldn't have cared less." He shrugged. "But then he decides it's in his best interest to retire, disappear. Apparently, he hadn't kept his 401(k) up to par so he asks me for money to keep his mouth shut about all those other kids. Bad decision. You see, I'm running for the state senate next year. I have big plans, Ms. Lane. I've made all the money I will ever need and now I want something else. Power and the kind of admiration that comes with it. Maybe I'll run for governor one day. Can't have this sort of thing cropping up in the news. You know how they like to dig up past sins on candidates."

The people who were hurt and murdered meant nothing to this man.

Killing her and Liam would be a mere nuisance for him.

The sound of a car door closing jerked her attention toward the dirt road.

Liam was here.

"It's about time," Burke muttered, his gaze focused in the direction of the road.

Halle ran.

She lunged deeper into the woods and darted first one direction and then the next. Burke screamed at her to stop but she kept going.

A shot rang out.

The bullet hit a tree not more than a few inches away from her.

She ducked and ran deeper to her left.

Another shot and then another.

Her heart was racing. Fear burned inside her but she didn't slow down. Ignored the limbs slapping at her face and her body.

She had to keep going.

Another shot.

She thought of the way Liam had looked at her this morning when he kissed her before heading to his hotel.

She thought of her parents.

A scream and then shouting echoed through the woods.

She skidded to a halt. Hid behind a tree. The voices were louder now.

"Halle!"

Liam.

She started to shout back at him but she was afraid that would only draw him closer to the trouble.

"Halle, it's okay," he shouted. "We've got him. You can come out now!"

"Ms. Lane!"

Was that...?

"This is Chief Brannigan, it's safe now."

Tears streaming down her cheeks and her heart pounding like a drum, she rushed toward the sound of their voices. She'd run so blindly and so fast from Burke she wasn't even sure how to get back to the dirt road.

Then she spotted Liam. She raced to him. His arms went around her.

"God almighty," he murmured against her ear, "I am so glad you're all right."

She drew back and smiled at him. "I am now."

Burke stared at her, his face red with fury. A plug was missing from the right sleeve of his jacket. The rip was soaked with blood.

"How did you know to come?" she asked the chief.

"Liam called me." He hitched his head toward the man holding her.

"I had no idea how to get to the road you mentioned and I couldn't make the damned navigation system in the rental work, so I called the chief. His was the only number I had. He knew the area and was suspicious. He wanted to come with me." Liam shifted his gaze to the chief. "I am very grateful he did."

"Thank you," Halle agreed.

Brannigan gave her a nod. "Thank *you*. It's always nice to take criminals off the street." He jerked Burke toward the road. "Let's go. I've got a car coming for you, Mr. Burke. Let's talk about your rights."

Liam hugged Halle again. She could feel his heart pounding in his chest.

When he drew back again, he smiled sadly. "Penelope and Claire are at your place. Penelope told me everything."

Halle swiped her eyes. "I'm sorry I caused all this to happen to you and your family."

"No." He touched her cheek. "You gave me the rest of my family. And I never want to lose you again."

He kissed her on the nose. "Now, let's get you home."

Chapter Sixteen

LATER

Saturday, June 20
Winchester

Halle stared at her reflection. The wedding dress fit like a glove. It was perfect.

Her mother appeared next to her. She smiled. "You look so beautiful, sweetheart. Now aren't you glad you didn't damage that dress when you sneaked it out of my keepsake trunk?"

Halle laughed, used the tip of her ring finger to swipe a tear from her eye before it messed up her makeup. "I sure am." She sighed. "I have waited to do this day right for a very long time."

"Twenty-five years."

Halle turned to face her mother. "I am so glad you and Dad want to move to Napa with us."

Her mother's face lit up. "Are you kidding? I've always dreamed of living in a Tuscan-style villa surrounded by vineyards. It's perfect, sweetie. It really is. I can't wait to spoil my grandchildren. And your father is determined to learn the art of winemaking from Liam."

Halle was so grateful there wouldn't be a trial. Burke had confessed to everything. He'd gone for a deal that kept him from getting a death sentence. Not only had he provided the information on all the children he and his minions had stolen, he'd provided the location of Liam's mother's remains, as well. A private service had been held in Napa last month and she had been buried next to his father.

They could all get on with the rest of their lives now.

Halle kissed her mother's cheek. "You're right. It's like a dream come true. A fairy tale that's finally getting its happy ending."

Her mother nodded. "The right ones always do."

The door opened and Claire slipped inside. She looked stunning in her maid-of-honor dress. "It's almost time."

Her dad stepped into the room next. "I'm not sure my heart can take the sheer beauty in this room."

Halle gave him a hug. "Let's do this."

Moments later as the wedding march played, Halle, holding her father's arm, walked up the aisle toward the man she had loved since she was a little girl.

He smiled at her and she knew without doubt that her mother was right. Some fairy tales did come true and this was one of them.

* * * * *

WE HOPE YOU ENJOYED
THIS BOOK FROM

H HARLEQUIN

INTRIGUE

Seek thrills. Solve crimes. Justice served.

Dive into action-packed stories that will keep you
on the edge of your seat. Solve the crime
and deliver justice at all costs.

6 NEW BOOKS AVAILABLE EVERY MONTH!

Annalise's heart beat so fast her stomach churned with nausea and an icy chill filled her veins. Bert was dead? The security guard with the great smile who loved to tell silly jokes was gone? And what two women had been killed? Who had been in the office at the time of this… this attack?

What were these killers doing here? What did they want?

The sound of distant sirens pierced the air. The big man cursed loudly.

"We were supposed to get in and out of here before the cops showed up," the tall, thin man said with barely suppressed desperation in his voice.

"Too late for that now," the big man replied. He turned and pointed his gun at Annalise. She stiffened. Was he going to kill her, as well? Was he going to shoot her right now? Kill the girls? She put her arms around her students and tried to pull them all behind her.

More sirens whirred and whooped, coming closer and closer.

"Don't move," he snarled at them. He took the butt of his gun and busted out one of the windows. The sound of the shattering glass followed by a rapid burst of gunfire out the window made her realize just how dangerous this situation was.

The police were outside. She and her students were inside with murderous gunmen, and she couldn't imagine how this all was going to end.

Don't miss
48 Hour Lockdown *by Carla Cassidy,*
available March 2020 wherever
Harlequin Intrigue books and ebooks are sold.

Harlequin.com